THE HAND THAT
SIGNED THE PAPER

Peter Murphy

Helen Demidenko was born in
Brisbane in 1971 and educated at
the University of Queensland,
where she read English and clas-
sics. She began writing short
stories and poetry while still in
high school and *The Hand that
Signed the Paper* is her first novel.

THE HAND THAT SIGNED THE PAPER

HELEN DEMIDENKO

ALLEN & UNWIN

Publication of this title was assisted by The Australia Council, the
Federal Government's arts funding and advisory body.

First published in 1994.
This edition published in 1995 by
Allen & Unwin Australia Pty Ltd
9 Atchison Street, St Leonards, NSW 2065 Australia

National Library of Australia
Cataloguing-in-Publication entry:

Demidenko, Helen, 1971– .
  The hand that signed the paper.

  ISBN 1 86448 018 1.

  I. Title.

A823.3

Set in 10/13 Palatino by DOCUPRO, Sydney
Printed by Australian Print Group, Maryborough, Victoria

10 9 8 7 6 5 4 3 2 1

For my family, and for Melissa Richards and Paul Gadaloff

Vox et praeterea nihil

AUTHOR'S NOTE

What follows is a work of fiction. The Kovalenko family depicted in this novel has no counterpart in reality. Nonetheless, it would be ridiculous to pretend that this book is unhistorical: I have used historical events and people where necessary throughout the text.

I would like to thank friends and family who talked with me, particularly Paul and Bronisław, who helped with translations and constructive criticism. I also wish to extend my thanks to Dr Con Castan, Department of English, University of Queensland, for his advice and support. Stories taken from many sources I have written, I hope, with love.

There are many stories in the world. People speak; stories are passed on. Stories and words have a life of their own, but only if others listen.

For the names of all places in Ukraine, I have used the more familiar Russian and Polish spellings. Below is an alphabetical list of key names found in this book and their correct Ukrainian spellings. For the names of people, I have used Ukrainian spellings. In Ukrainian, the letter 'g' is usually pronounced softly, as an 'h'.

Familiar usage	*Ukrainian*
Berdichev	Berdychiv
Dnieper	Dnipro
Kharkov	Kharkiv
Khmel'nik	Khmel'nyts'kyy
Kiev	Kiyiv
L'vóv	L'viv
Tarnopol	Ternopil'
Vinnitsa	Vynnytsya

ACKNOWLEDGMENTS

The author and publisher wish to thank the following for permission to quote copyright material:

J.M. Dent for an extract from the poem 'The Hand that Signed the Paper' by Dylan Thomas, published in *Dylan Thomas Collected Poems* J.M. Dent, 1957.

While every effort has been made to trace copyright holders whose work is used in this book, any further information is welcomed by the author and the publisher.

The hand that signed the paper felled a city;
Five sovereign fingers taxed the breath,
Doubled the globe of dead and halved a country;
These five kings did a king to death.

The hand that signed the treaty bred a fever,
And famine grew, and locusts came;
Great is the hand that holds dominion over
Man by a scribbled name.

Dylan Thomas, *The Hand that Signed the Paper*

In such condition. . .there is no Knowledge of the face of the Earth; no account of Time; no Arts; no Letters; no Society; and which is worst of all, continuall feare, and danger of violent death: And the life of man, solitary, poore, nasty, brutish, and short.

Thomas Hobbes, *Leviathan*

ONE

As I drive down the Pacific Highway, the French are busy dropping bombs into the waters in which my nieces swim, the Americans and Iraqis are engaged in a bizarre competition to see who can destroy the world many times over most, and my uncle will soon be on trial for war crimes and crimes against humanity. I wonder casually, as I turn off the main road to fill up with petrol, if Eichmann had a daughter and if she felt the same way as I do now. It is an idle question, but I toy with it as the light and darkness at sunset plays over the glittering Ampol sign. This is one petrol station where they still serve you while you sit in your car. A pimply boy walks towards me across the asphalt and asks 'how much?' and I say 'twenty dollars'. I sit in the cockpit of my car, and look at my watch. The boy takes my keys. The key ring has a cheap plastic figurine of 'Expo Oz' attached. I've had it for four years, and Expo Oz's platypus bill now has very little paint left on it.

Right now, I am missing my Set Theory and Logic lecture, and will soon miss my Modern Political Ideologies lecture. I left home earlier this morning, giving Cathe a week's rent and telling her that I was 'going to drive down the coast to see about my uncle'. Cathe—and a few other of my close friends—know that I am related to the Kovalenko who has recently been charged with war crimes. That in itself is no guarantee of a trial, but the fear is real. I have confirmed to Cathe that the charges are true, and that the family is in the process of engaging a lawyer.

When news of the trials first began, I would sit beside the radio listening to 'PM' with the sort of focus I really needed for my university studies. Cathe would look worried and bring me cups of hot chocolate.

'Is he in trouble?' she asked once. 'I mean, is it serious enough to send him to gaol?'

'I don't know. When uncle Vitaly first heard about the trials, he hid under the kitchen table. Staciya came home from the shops and found him hugging the table leg and yelling "the Israelis are coming to get me!". It was funny, at the time. He could be in trouble, I suppose. I don't know. No one in our family knows about the law, the legal system, anything like that. We've got two doctors, a builder and an architect. No lawyers.'

Cathe laughed. 'I hope Staciya got him out from under the table.'

'He came out to eat, don't worry.'

Later that night, after Cathe had gone to bed, I thought about Vitaly and the trial. It seemed strangely distant; distant and silent. Silent. A silent movie. I felt angry in a vague, unspecific way. About the trials. About the furtiveness I was sure existed in my own family. I rolled a cigarette, lit it and sat out on the verandah. It was raining and the timber beneath my bare feet was cool and sloppy. The smoke and the damp kept the mosquitoes away. I watched the rain bead and collect in black puddles on the concrete footpath below. The legal system, I thought. It's too big to deal with, too big to comprehend.

I did not tell Cathe that my father could be in as much 'trouble' as Vitaly. My father was just a boy, four years younger than Vitaly. I did not tell Cathe about the hate, or how the Ukrainian famine bled into the Holocaust and one fed the other. All the things I never told.

The figures meant nothing. I needed to think of my great-aunt and her twelve children. My best friend at school whose grandmother died in Auschwitz. Only then did the statistics acquire faces, histories, personal likes and dislikes. By that stage my stomach usually took on a doughy, frightened feel. The news was full of Somalia and Bosnia; the colour images still flicker and haunt. Two Serbs wipe their feet on the Croatian flag. A sad little village nestled between soft green hills burns. Two lean black men drag the naked, punctured body of a US marine down a dusty street.

I pull my legs up under my chin while the Ampol boy brings me my change. He gives me thirty dollars. 'Going down to the Indy Car Grand Prix?' he asks. I shake my head. 'Don't have enough money,' I say. 'I'm seeing rellies. I'm not into car racing, much.'

My father is unhurried still in his movements, but he scowls and scratches his face. 'I am an Australian citizen,' he says. 'I'm all Australian now. I've worked so hard to be Australian. . .' I have spoken about this with him, but nothing argumentative has ever come of it. I ask him about these trials, about his brother, what he thinks. He shrugs his shoulders. He is ordinary and quiet. 'You don't know what it was like. It was a crazy time. People did things, and you. . .you can't explain them now.'

It is only when I see material evidence of events that I think of him differently. He is one of the unprosecuted; he was the youngest. He is my father.

I look up into the sun, squinting. I am wearing tinted prescription John Lennon glasses, and I remember my uncle's comment when I first wore them home from the optometrist. I was 15, and John Lennon was God. 'Ha,' he said, 'if it wasn't for John Lennon, those'd still be Heinrich Himmler glasses,' I remember laughing.

3

I began to discover in upper primary what my uncle and father 'did' in the war; it was one of those things. I wasn't a Nazi. None of my family were Nazis. We weren't Germans. People just did certain things that could not be prevented. We were a typical enough family, although more political than most. My father voted DLP. I supported the Labor Party. I never argued about politics with my father. He didn't care. I even helped the local branch with handing out how-to-vote cards on various polling days, and the local member once gave me a job reference. I did not get the job, but that wasn't his fault.

My mother was the true right-winger. She was a member of the National Party of Australia, Queensland Branch, and also handed out how-to-votes on polling day. Out of deference to such family division, on polling day the Liberals always obligingly set up their stall in between the Labor and National stalls. 'Between the warring Kovalenkos' one Liberal candidate commented wryly. Mother and I would glare malevolently at each other for the duration of voting, and then ride home in the same car. But my mother's politics were excused. She was Protestant Irish, and believed in the flag and the Queen and such things.

I contacted her from the University, from the public phone located under the sandstone Forgan Smith Building. 'I've got to see Uncle Vitaly,' I said. I know that she nodded, and partly covered the receiver with her hand, stifling sobs. 'It's something that you want to do,' she said.

Cathe nodded solemnly when I told her. 'I thought you would. He's your uncle.' She laughed ruefully. 'You'll miss the Medieval Ball, though.' I laughed. 'I shall blot my perfect record.' She took me by the shoulders. 'I want you to understand. . .that. . .that I think it's wrong to try them. That trying people for what they did in a war legitimises other wartime activities that are left untried. War is a crime, of itself. So I really hope that nothing comes of this, and everything just blows over.' Her words comforted me for a moment, and I left the house surrounded by a wonderful sense of calm. It was only later, as I drove towards the coast, that I began to cry.

The sunlight slants more precipitously, behind me an angry driver honks his horn. He wants the pump. I sit in the sun-warmed car briefly before starting it and driving along the access road onto the highway. I turn on the radio; the Logan FM station plays 'Under the Bridge'. 'I don't ever wanna feel. . .how I felt that day. . .take me to the place I love. . .take me all the way.' I wipe my eye. That song, for some reason, always makes me think of what my family did. 'Under the bridge downtown. . .is where I drew some blood. . .Under the bridge downtown. . .I could not get enough.'

Vitaly did unspeakable things. I have known about these things for some time now. How poor and hungry Ukrainians shot Jews for bread and sausage and vodka. How my father and my uncle became part of the machinery of the Holocaust. How my aunt married a senior SS officer. How people slaughtered without compunction. My brother Bret went to Vietnam, and came back nearly mad from what he did, with dreams about little gook children pocked with bullets and Vietnamese girls raped by both Americans and Vietcong. My father is sane. So are Vitaly and aunt Kateryna. None of them mad. Not now. Not one.

Near Babii-Yar, a deep, sandy gorge, the Dnieper flowed under a bridge. This deep ravine that marked out a tributary of the great river was perfect for what the Germans wanted. Just perfect.

I discovered the past when I was twelve. It was summer; next year I would start high school. I lay on the cool floor of our air-conditioned lounge, watching cricket. My parents were at the weekend markets, and I was burnt from spending the previous day in the sun. I had a sudden desire to locate the family Rubik's cube, and spent the next half-hour searching energetically for it. Not on tiptoes in my cupboard. Not downstairs. Not buried beneath the reams of paper that littered the dining table.

Finally, I found it in the top drawer of my father's bedside table, in a place where I never normally ventured, beneath several fat envelopes. The envelopes were stuffed with old photographs. I hurriedly pulled the cube from the drawer and the contents of the envelopes spilled onto the floor and over the bed. The photos were the box brownie type for the most part—small, sepia, and delineated around the margins with a white border. A few were larger—handsome black-and-white studio shots of my uncle. My father. My aunt Kateryna beside an unknown man with white blond hair. The man had a handsome, wicked face.

All the men were clothed in a black uniform marked at the collar with the runic insignia of the SS. I abandoned the Rubik's cube in the drawer. Hurrying, I spread the pictures over the bed. The big pretty ones to one side. The little ones I tipped from the envelopes. In one, a group shot, a tall, expressionless man stood beside a youthful group of SS that included my uncle and my father. Their uniforms looked new and starched. They grinned at the camera, even though their officer did not. In front of them, a large machine-gun was set up on tripod legs. One crouched beside it. Its lethal muzzle ended somewhere outside the photograph. In another, uncle Vitaly sat at the end of a long ditch, a machine-gun across his knees, his hands draped over it, his legs hanging into the pit. He stared insolently out at me, a lock of white hair over one eye. The shot was underexposed, and I could not see what was in the ditch. Other pictures made up for this lack. Pits choked with bodies. Grinning men waving a flag that I later learned was the flag of the Ukraine. A photograph of a big factory with low timber buildings surrounded by barbed wire and pine brush. My uncle before the carved factory gates. My

6

aunt in a smart wartime dress and hairdo beside the wicked-looking man. Beside them a chart with maps on it clipped to a board. A poor-looking man with a big star around his neck, being chased up the street by an SS man wielding a rifle with deadly intent. My father. My Father.

THE PAST, someone has said, is another country, foreign, strangely inviting, beautiful. Other people live there, not us, so we are safe from it. There is our past, the stuff of gory war films—bad Hollywood, if you will. The nasty ones are in there, in the movies, at least. Mixed in with Shirley Temple and Bogart and Kate Hepburn. Extras mainly, not people, with helmets low down over their eyes so that you cannot see their faces. They drag Jews out of trains, shove them into gas chambers, line them up and shoot them. They are usually given one line—a barking *'Schnell, schnell, schneller. . .los, los'*— then they obligingly disappear. It's good that they do: we are interested in the people who made the bullets, not the people who fired them. The latter make us uncomfortable, because, if we look too closely, we see sad eyes and tragic fates. They do these things because we believe they are savage people. They keep doing them because such savagery is endemic. They can wear a brutal mask easily. It feels good for the viewer that they seem to believe in their own savageness. At least, then, the two—watched and watching—cannot be confused, separated as they are by both time and appearance.

KATERYNA: During the spring of 1933, there was no seed to plant for the wheat, no fodder for the animals; the communists had come to our village and taken it all in the previous year. People starved, and the streets of the capital were not the only streets strewn with the bodies of starving Ukrainians. Every village had a pile of fresh bodies awaiting burial each morning. The communists and Jews would step over them, eyes averted, on their way to work. Sometimes people would be shot by the communists for speaking in Ukrainian, but this was rare by comparison. Mostly the famine did its quiet work, and only kulaks were shot. The land, they told us, would then belong to everybody. In the beginning kulaks were defined as rich farmers, but after a while, 'kulak' meant any land-holder, then any crop-grower, and finally any Ukrainian. Executions were frequent. But the famine was always the fastest executioner, even after the communists and their organised Cheka came and took people—politicals and Petlyura supporters—away for the transports to Siberia. This was for resettlement, we were told, and no one ever saw them again.

The dusty summer spread out under the bowl of the sky, and potbellied children sat in the unpaved streets, clothed in a cloak of flies. The Ukraine has a deserved reputation for cold, but in these years, summer and famine were inextricably linked. Children were born dead, or only lived for a few hours in the hungry, sweating heat. Those who grew were never sent to school. The communists had given up sending us to school; we refused to learn the lessons they had to teach, and jokes about 'stupid Ukrainians' were very popular in Moscow then. Students in one high school lynched the teacher who beat them for speaking Ukrainian. For this, the entire village was deported. 'The removal of dangerous Nationalists', it was called.

Skilfully, the communists hid their famine from the world, and all the visiting trade union leaders on junkets from Australia and America and Britain were shown only the successful kolkhozes around Moscow. In the maps supplied to them, the Ukraine was a white void—not even Kiev was marked. They returned to their own countries to champion the land of the proletariat, while our people starved. People have since wondered why we did not do more to resist, but it was very hard for us. Millions of us died in the famine. Carefully, they starved away our desire for national independence. The communists had both the money and the guns; we had neither. But, people reasoned, if someone were to come and give us either or both, then we would take revenge. Unholy, Godless and bloody revenge. We would kill every communist and Jew in the Ukraine.

But I should tell you that we were not always bitter like this. The bitterness came slowly. We did not always starve, although we were always poor. Most of the time, we were able to tiptoe through our valley of sorrows upside down and imagine it a merry place. Things were no better or no worse after the first coming of the Bolsheviks, even though some people said that the sky would fall because of the terrible sacrilege of Godless atheists ruling Ukraine.

Comrade Lenin broke up the largest estates, and gave even the poorest peasants some land. Nationalists and Democrats were shot, but they lived in the cities. If you were peasants like us, in the villages around Khmel'nik, you were safe if you kept quiet. In those days we had tremendous family gatherings, and I remember people coming to our farm from as far as Vinnitsa and Berdichev for an important event such as a wedding. My aunt Ludmylla and her husband Serhiy and their twelve children, my cousins, as well as my grandparents would come. Because my mother had only three children, Ludmylla would say blessings and prayers, and hope that some of her good fortune would rub off on 'poor Natasha'. People danced. The women made beautiful things to eat, the men wore their best pairs of polished *choboty*. Little wooden toys would be carved for the children: beautiful toys that proved that Ukrainian craftsmen are so skilled that they truly can carve a spoon with an axe. My father and my uncle taught Vitaly to dance—I remember the three of them tripping lightly through the long grass. Vitaly was a very good dancer, even as a boy. Strong and quick and graceful.

So, for this period, the communists left us alone. There was balance in the world. A little peace, enough prosperity to ensure a good wedding party at least. Only my father was sceptical. Often he would tell us to engrave the appearance of Ukraine somewhere permanent on our hearts, so that we could always call on it if we were deported: the time will come, he said, when the engraving will be all that you have. But people didn't understand his scepticism. They considered his warnings morbid, out of step with the times.

This is why what followed came so suddenly. One year, all of my cousins visited to celebrate the wedding of my father's youngest sister. Two years later, all twelve children were dead. Comrade Stalin and Comrade Kaganovich, so little known to the Soviet peoples while Lenin was alive, became strangely prominent. It is hard to describe this change. At first, worshipping God was forbidden. If you were caught, you were shot. People who spoke only Ukrainian were thrown out of their jobs. Our land was requisitioned, and resistance was out of the question. In my village a group of about twenty farmers refused to give up their crop to the NKVD men who had been sent to collect it. They armed themselves with scythes and rakes. I shall never forget what followed. The NKVD came with a flamethrower and two machine-guns, chained all of these men together and locked them in a barn. Then they set fire to the barn. We had been ordered into our homes, but we could still hear the screams.

This was how the hate started. As the years passed, the hate got worse. I didn't see all of it because I was sent away to Komsomol school, but my brothers Evheny and Vitaly saw it, lived through it. But I have to say that I saw the beginning, in the main street of Khmel'nik, a little town like any other little town, choked with queues of tired, hungry people.

THE LETTERS 'SMERSH' stand, in Russian, for the words 'death to spies'. SMERSH men and women come into the town of Khmel'nik and arrest a certain Fyodor Kovalenko for the crime of *nationalist subversion*. We don't know if this is a real crime, or only a fiction. They take him to the building that used to be a prison in Tsarist times. Now it has been converted into SMERSH offices. In the Civil War, Fyodor Kovalenko gave shelter to two fleeing officers of the White Army. The two men fled to Siberia. One escaped to Nationalist China, finally reaching Australia. The other lay low, and was eventually captured in Yakutia by NKVD in the winter of 1933.

After six weeks of having his skull fractured, his balls crushed, his fingers cut off, he finally tells who aided him in his flight. So the SMERSH people come down to starving Khmel'nik to arrest Fyodor Kovalenko, farmer and nationalist subversive, who has been expecting them. He realises that he has no hope of survival, that he will be shot here or will perish in Archangelsk, so, as they arrest him, he resists, shouting as he is dragged down the summer street, past the potbellied children, the women laden with firewood. Fyodor was once a big, healthy Ukrainian, a fine baritone in the church choir. For a long time his voice was lowered to a whisper. Now he shouts, waving spindly arms. My brother and I each hold one of our mother's hands. Vitaly is twelve. I am ten. Evheny is eight, and at home on the collective. My mother is pregnant. She says nothing. She queues quietly, waiting for bread. My father is shouting. 'Long Live Petlyura! Long Live the Ukraine! God Bless President Roosevelt! May he blow Comrade Stalin off the map!' He says the most inflammatory things possible. 'Fight, you people. You don't have to accept this! Fight! Fight! Fight Marx and the fucking Jewish

Bolsheviks! Fight!' My parents came into town to queue for different items. One in each queue, so that more food could be acquired. Mother says nothing. Vitaly says 'I will fight'. 'Not now,' says my mother. My father goes, unquietly, raging. He is not by nature an angry man, and the little that I recall of him revolves around his soft voice, the sweet tobacco smell that lingers in his white whiskers. The shouting startles me, and people stare silently at my father and the two SMERSH men from their places in various queues. He had many relatives in Khmel'nik. Others were also taken, by famine, by SMERSH, by shootings in the streets. This was how the hate grew.

AFTER A while, we began to hear about Adolf Hitler, and wild stories started to circulate. How everybody in Germany had enough to eat, and that they all had telephones and automobiles and radio sets. The communists at first denied the truth of all of this, saying that Hitler was an evil capitalist, but later, they began to say good things about him: that he had provided everyone with jobs, that the workers were happy. We accepted without question the revised opinion of Herr Hitler. People had learnt by now that the communists changed their minds on the slightest pretext.

This did not stop them from deporting many of the Volksdeutsche to Siberia. The Volksdeutsche had lived in Ukraine since the time of Catherine. She had imported them to make Russia look like Europe; she needed their nimble, skilled fingers, their intelligence. She needed them to drag Russia 'kicking and screaming' into modernity. Being German herself, she did not like Russia as it was: she could take comfort from her own people. When they had done the tasks set them, she let them settle in Ukraine and Poland. They settled.

Now anyone with a German name—even if his German blood had been almost completely diluted by Ukrainian—was at risk. Some hid their language and their names and tried to stay in the villages; many were drafted into the Red Army, where it was hoped they could be made into communists. Comrade Stalin would regret this later, as they all changed sides when captured by the Nazis. Others were simply removed to Soviet Central Asia, to perish among the Tartars and the Tajiks, people both unlovely and unlovable to Comrade Stalin in Moscow. People watched, in Khmel'nik, as the town's Volksdeutsche were put in boxcars and directed towards Vinnitsa, and thence to West Siberia. They looked at us sadly, shaking their heads. We wanted to help them, give them food. Already, in the city, they could see what had once belonged to them being given to Russian and Jewish colonists. Nothing was given to their Ukrainian neighbours. This was considered too dangerous. SMERSH shot a woman on the railway platform who tried to give a Volksdeutsche woman she knew some black bread and sausage. Her blood trickled over the cement, slow in the cold winter air, as the train pulled away.

We starved less in the late thirties, and Comrade Stalin saw fit to come down to the Ukraine and bribe us with candies to support the party. But he still wanted our wings broken, speaking our language in a public place was still difficult. SMERSH still visited our poor country with worrying regularity. Even communists were not safe: purges were conducted, and sometimes the most loyal party members would be arrested. I think that SMERSH also had a quota, and once they ran out of kulaks they were forced to take their own.

Thousands upon thousands of Ukrainian children were also taken from their parents and sent to Komsomol schools, sometimes when they were only infants. When they were taken this young, they forgot their land and their mother tongue. I too was enrolled as a Komsomol, and was taken away from my mother as much as possible. The communists felt that if you separated us from our religion and our stories, from the beliefs that defined us as Ukrainians, eventually you would make us merely good communists, good Russians. Eventually you would assimilate us, Russify us, make us like everyone else. This did not work with the older children. Besides, the communists did not want to educate too many Ukrainians too well, in case they worked out how to overthrow the system.

My brother Evheny ran away from the school, Vitaly never came. Vitaly stayed on the kolkhoz, as a farmer, and never learnt to read and write. This upset him, and he would lightly brush the front page of *Pravda* with his long fingers, reverently, as if it contained within an absolute truth that might be acquired by some sort of osmosis.

At the school the communists told lies about Petlyura, our hero, who had briefly led an independent Ukraine in 1918. Petlyura had tried very hard to establish a genuinely democratic government in the teeth of Bolshevik opposition. He tried to encourage cultural respect, ethnic peace. He tried to distribute land more fairly among the peasants. He fought against both Red and White with everything he had. He and his compatriots took to the low Dnieper hills and hid by the serpentine rivers and in the thick forests. They struggled. They lost.

They said he was a counter-revolutionary and a traitor to the worker. I explained that the Ukraine did not have workers then, only farmers, and that Petlyura was good for the farmers. I was beaten with a birch switch in front of my fellow students, and told that the peasants had to become workers now, because the peasants were always counter-revolutionaries. I was left to sit outside, and was told that I could have as many candies as I wanted if I would renounce my opinion about Petlyura. It was winter, and minus fifteen degrees Celsius. It was not snowing, but the wind from the north was sharp and bitter. I sat on the steps that led to the low, whitewashed building that housed our school for three and a half hours. I refused to move or change my opinion when the cadre leader poked her head around the door.

The famine had killed my little brother, Anatoly. I remember how he was shrivelled even as a baby, when he should have been healthy and pink. Fierce green eyes stared wide from his tiny face, but he did not have the strength to cry. My mother went to the kommissar's house, to beg for milk as her breasts had none. The kommissar was not home, but his wife—a Jewish doctor—was. She sent out a guard, then came herself. She said it would be good if a few more of us died, there were so many. We bred like yard dogs. My mother begged for some medicine. Anatoly was so sick now he had to have medicine. Mrs Kommissar refused. 'I am a physician, not a veterinarian,' she said softly, enunciating the words with a kind of feral sharpness. 'Get away.'

I hugged my knees tightly after the third hour. The cold had developed a numbing quality, and I knew that I would have to give in soon. Besides, the prospect of candies was beginning to sound inviting. I had missed lunch, and dinner hour was drawing near. My teeth chattered. The cadre leader appeared for the fifth time. 'Kateryna Kovalenko, will you renounce your opinion about Petlyura and the farmers, and let Comrade Stalin give you candies?' I stood up and began slowly to inch inside. A blast of warm air stung my face. 'I take it that this means "yes"?' I nodded glumly. My hands were sore inside my gloves. I looked at her sullenly, and she must have wondered why the people here hated her so. She—a Jewess from Leningrad—would never understand. We were just 'Ukrainian fascists', to be bent to the new system. In all probability, she could not understand why communism was not automatically bringing prosperity to the peasants. She no doubt blamed the peasants. She looked at me, almost kindly, brown eyes gleaming. 'Do you believe in God, Kateryna Kovalenko?' I answered 'yes' without hesitation. I had caused so much trouble in the 'History of the Revolution' class that a little more would do no harm. 'Why? God does you no good.'

'Yes, but you do us harm. You starve us. You steal our crops. You killed my brother.'

She was startled at the hatred that came from this thirteen-year-old child, and she became defensive. 'I didn't personally. You must understand that.'

The cold and the revulsion got the better of me suddenly. I shouted. I shouted so that every person in the entire building heard what I said. 'Yes you did, you filthy fucking Bolshevist. You and all the filthy fucking Jewish Bolshevists. Marx. Trotsky. Kamenev. Kaganovich. Bukharin. Fuck you! And fuck Comrade Stalin! Fuck him!' This angry reminder of Tsarist times terrified her momentarily. I was an unarmed thirteen-year-old girl, but for an instant, I became the master of the Black Hundreds, leading a mob of sabre-wielding Cossacks into the *shtetl*. She blanched, baulked, then grabbed me by my long plaits and began to hit me. 'Ukrainian fascist! Ukrainian fascist!' She twisted my hair around her arm, immobilising me, and continued to strike. My mouth was bleeding, and she broke my nose. Students and teachers, attracted by the commotion, poured into the room, my brother among them. One of the male cadre leaders helped her administer the hiding, hitting me with his belt. I screamed, this time for help. 'They're killing me! They're killing me! Help me!' The students—nearly all Ukrainians—stood around in dumb anguish, wringing their hands and fiddling with their red Komsomol scarves. They looked down at the timber floor, and bit their lips.

Finally, the two cadre leaders dumped me on my back, and I lay in an expanding pool of blood. 'Look,' said the Jewess from Leningrad. 'How like cattle the Ukrainians are—they do nothing.' The man agreed, and jested briefly with one of the soldiers who guarded our school. 'Stupid,' he said to the soldier, who smiled weakly, his eyes narrow and wet. 'Just plain stupid.' He kicked me in the side as I lay there, and, smiling at the soldier, ordered the students away. Evheny stood a moment longer, blinking, tears running down his smooth face.

During the night, and well after dinner, I tried to move. The floor was sodden and sticky, and my side creaked strangely. I propped myself on my elbows, and tried to rise, but the room reeled crazily and I let myself slowly sink. The school was silent, bathed in darkness. Cold seeped under the door; it was snowing outside. I tried to move into a more comfortable position, but was startled and fearful when footfalls echoed in my direction, finally stopping behind me. I began to cry. 'Please don't hurt me. I take back everything I said. Just don't hurt me anymore. Please.' The soldier who had seemed less than enthusiastic in his approval of the cadre leaders' activities bent down in front of me, stroking my encrusted face. His cheeks were streaked with tears. 'I'm so sorry. So sorry. Oh, God in Heaven. I am Ukrainian and Kalmyk. Please forgive me. Forgive me.' His last few words drowned in phlegm, and, as gently as he could manage, he gathered me up and stood upright. I lolled, a dead weight in his arms, as he took me to the infirmary.

Carefully, he seemed to collect his wits, and before he knocked to wake the doctor, he looked at me. 'My name is Shura. I am your friend. One day we will get these bastards. Hitler will help us. You wait and see.'

He told the doctor that I had repented of my opinions; he told her a long story about my supposed attachment to communism, and said that I was unwell when I made my earlier remarks. He was trusted, evidently; the doctor believed every word, her face breaking into a gimmicky, trusting grin. She washed me and dressed my wounds, then tucked me into a soft bed and stuck tubes up my nose. When she was behind the partition that separated her quarters from the infirmary, Shura crouched beside me, whispering. His fingers brushed my face. He smiled so that his narrow, Mongol eyes almost closed. He said nothing important, nothing I could understand. I wanted him to stay, but he rose and left, without looking behind him.

VITALY stood up slowly, massaging his back. The tractor had broken down, and they were scything again, bringing the wheat in by hand. He looked towards the stream that marked the boundary of the collective. The tractor lay partly buried in sand; when it had broken down, the driver had assumed that that was it, and had wandered slowly home, shrugging his shoulders and complaining about newfangled machinery. During the night there had been a flash flood, and now the tractor was buried, and probably irretrievable. Vitaly sat carefully, parting the fresh stubble with his hands. It was clean and spare, his country, and the sun gleamed on the yet to be harvested crop. Gold and blue, the colours of the Ukraine, he thought. How well chosen they were. He looked at the flushed clean stream again, and considered the risks involved in taking a swim and shirking the afternoon's labour. The kommissar had been lax in the last few weeks—he was Ukrainian himself, and drank too much vodka. Vitaly supposed that he felt sorry for his own, but he was still given to wild mood swings and drunken rages.

The party bosses from Kiev were stunned to learn that the harvest was progressing just as quickly without the tractor, although they shook their heads when the kommissar told them that only three girls and one boy from the whole collective were attending Komsomol school. Vitaly peeled off his shirt and used it as a pillow for his neck and back, spreading it on the stubble. He folded his hands under his head, and looked up. Two hawks wheeled and circled far above him, screeching. The authorities had dragged little Evheny away to be a Komsomol student in the spring: he was only small, and too young to help with anything. Kateryna was gone too: she was clever, they said. She could already read and write. Vitaly was pleased that he did not have to go to school, even though he would have liked to learn how to read and write. Now he could pursue his interest in Ulrike Uhrman, the Volksdeutsche from Russia. She had lovely round breasts, and yesterday she had let him hold them in his hands.

One of the hawks seemed to chase the other, briefly, then they turned and circled again.

'Ay! Vitaly! piss-head's coming!' Vitaly jumped up, startled, and began to put on his shirt. He saw Barsek Ohlobla, ostensibly the supervisor, sprint towards him from the river, dripping wet. Someone else thought swimming in such heat was good for the soul, obviously. Barsek was yelling. 'It's the boss. He's pissed as a Pan, and he's got a whip.'

Vitaly whistled with surprise, a screeching, penetrating blast that mingled with the sound of the hawks above. 'I thought he'd given that away. He's been good lately.'

Barsek drew level with him. 'No, not him. He's shitty because the boy they took to school's come back. He's run away.' Barsek puffed. 'He's over in the field behind that buggered tractor. See.' He pointed.

'That's my brother! The fucker's chasing my brother!'

Barsek had not properly seen the quarry in the unharvested crop, and now he watched as the wheat parted, allowing a small figure to disappear into the bushes that fringed the stream. 'My brother! That's Evheny!' Vitaly sprinted over the lion-coloured stubble towards the water, shouting, 'Evheny! Evheny!'

'Vitaly! Don't. . .shit, he's mad as fuck, don't do it!'

Barsek ran awkwardly, the stubble stinging his bare feet. He had ignored it before, and now it bit and prickled. Vitaly splashed into the water, meeting his brother halfway. He swept him up in his arms, laughing. 'Home! You've come home!'

Barsek pulled up beside him. 'Where's piss-head? He was here. . .I saw him. I swear I did.'

He looked across at the opposing bank. The drunken kommissar lay awkwardly in the mud, hands covering his face. The whip handle was wedged in the root of a shrub, with the lash floating in the clear water, like a monstrous eel. He cried noisily, big vodka tears leaking out between his fingers as he sat up. He looked at Evheny, his sad, red face covered with apology. Tufts of grey hair protruded from his ears, and his eyebrows met in the middle. He smiled and mumbled something, but his voice was too thick with grog and tears to make what he said coherent.

The school never tried to retrieve Evheny Kovalenko, and his chief task was now the reading of stories to the others of an evening. Besides him, only the kommissar and his wife could read, and frequently he was too drunk, and she too arrogant, so the boy's childish voice would come seeping out of window cracks and door jambs, would waft down between the houses. It was cold now, and he missed his poor, beaten sister. She had given him some food and a stolen compass from the pioneer's storehouse at the school, and he fled late one evening. An Asian-looking soldier known to him only as Shura had seen him, but waved him on, smiling.

He had travelled through several large towns. One had a landscaped park with a war memorial and fountain. A little sign hung before the chain that marked its perimeter: 'No Ukrainians and no dogs allowed in this park'. He had hidden in the park for a night, where no one would suspect a small boy in the neat uniform of a Komsomol school, all the while he did not speak and let his accent reveal his identity. He listened to the conversation of the Russian colonists who sometimes walked past the fountain. On the fringes of this town, he passed the fibro shanties where the Ukrainians lived, saw their snotty-nosed children with filthy, matted hair sitting in the mud. He watched as a small child and a scabrous dog of all breeds fought over possession of a bone, tugging and grunting. Observe that. The entrances and exits.

An elderly Jew gave him some food in the second town he came to. He noticed that the town's synagogue had been converted into a revolutionary museum, and that NKVD troops stood guard to keep the Orthodox Jews away from what had once been their place of worship. A red and black banner obscured the Star of David on the roof. 'Celebrate what Communism does to free the Jews!', it read. The NKVD troops distributed food parcels to the Jews who came by, and a queue developed, but no Jews were allowed inside. Some Ukrainians tried to line up for food as well, but an NKVD man shot two of them, and ordered their bodies to be taken away.

The old Jew bent over Evheny, kindly. 'Run along, little communist,' he said, 'and take this with you.' He gave him a small parcel containing bread and cheese and some butter. Evheny stood clutching the parcel as the black-robed old man walked stiffly and nobly away from him down the street. He sat on the curb, eating guiltily. His mother said that Jews polluted everything they touched, but he was hungry.

Vitaly remembered his sister when Evheny read poetry. Vitaly said to Barsek that he could hear the boy's heart breaking, because he said the words so well. Barsek was afraid now. Vitaly said he wanted to kill his enemies, and his eyes were cold and clear and bright when he spoke. Barsek secretly prayed to Mary Mother of Jesus that some love would come to the collective, before Vitaly forgot what it meant and just hated. One evening, in mid-winter, Vitaly found a hawk frozen dead in the yard behind the equipment shed. He buried it carefully, remembering the hawks in summer.

Later he found the bodies of six local kulaks who could read. The communists had come to the village calling for literate volunteers; the communists had said that they were needed for important work in Kiev. Only literate people need apply. They were very pleasant and encouraging, so despite what the communists had done to kulaks and suspected kulaks in the past, six volunteered for the work. The communists took them away in the back of a green army lorry. Vitaly found them under the river ice, after cutting out a round hole through which he intended to fish. Their lips were blue, their eyes bleedy and bulbous. He ran home panting, fishless, crying and sobbing.

Shortly after this, officials from Kiev finally came to fix and retrieve the broken-down tractor, and took the man responsible for its abandonment away with them. Vanya the poor drunken kommissar tried to explain that the flash flood had occurred because all the trees further upstream had been felled, but the communists would not listen, insisting that the farmer was a saboteur.

Short, muscular Nikolai Manchuk found the body two days later, mutilated and frozen, but still clearly recognisable. His eyes had been gouged out and his nose cut off, but they had left his dark, bushy moustache intact. Nikolai dragged the body seven kilometres, depositing it on the kommissar's doorstep, before returning home to his young wife, shaking with cold and anger. The kommissar's wife Doctor Judit spat on him as he left, and he let the warm globule on his fur cap harden in the cold before he scraped it away. He did not turn to look at her once, but continued his slow, angry walk through the village. Inside, the kommissar mumbled drunkenly. 'We're goinggg mmm to get it, you know. One day they'll get fed umm up and kill us all. Kill us all. All of us.'

She turned sharply, rounding on him. 'Rubbish, Vanya. Comrade Stalin will protect us.'

JUDIT: Dear Mother,
I am writing to you because I am so alone here. I write every day but now I need someone to write to, so I have to write to you. I hate this country and these people. Vanya becomes

more Ukrainian and less Soviet each day. He drinks all the time, like the foolish villagers. It has got so that he cannot appear in public without disgracing himself in some way. I am also concerned that he is making himself worse by sneaking into my medical stores at night and stealing medicines. I notice that bottles are missing but I never see him do it.

The country itself is so flat, so predictable. There are no hills like at home. There are little scrubby trees with no flowers, and the colours of the seasons do not vary in the slightest. Vanya said Little Russia was beautiful, and he speaks of it long and lovingly, but I cannot see it. I have tried to see it but I just can't. At first I thought that there was something wrong with me, that I would learn, but it doesn't seem to be that way.

If only I could describe the village to you—but there is so little to describe. There is one muddy street, with a few poor houses on each side. One farm sports a nice airy barn, with swept floors, so the young people meet there regularly. I am sure it is where most of the children are conceived. There is a little wooden church with bright ikons inside and gilt over the door. I have tried to explain to these people that it is the church that keeps them poor, but they will not listen, so I have had to put whitewash over the ikons and close the church. Vanya says this will make them even less willing to work.

When I was at the medical school in Moscow I did not believe that such people existed, except in Gogol's stories, yet my betrothed came from this place! Vanya was a fine exotic Cossack at the university—but here, here he is just a drunken peasant. He abuses me for not understanding his people, and says that one day they will take revenge. I tell him that they are too indolent for revenge, but he won't accept it. I cannot believe that people will do nothing to improve themselves. When they get the chance, they drink first and then sleep, grunting like pigs. They do not want to use the modern equipment—the harvesters and the tractors. I try to explain that they will be able to grow more crops, and contribute more to the quota. But they prefer their horse-drawn ploughs and want to grow legumes for half the year, or let the fields lie fallow. They bring starvation on themselves.

They breed like true Catholics: the women are either nursing or in pup, without any variation. They are terrified of the evil eye, and constantly have visions of saints and spirits. I have tried to tell them that women are to be liberated from slavery in the Soviet Union, and that this is what Comrade Lenin and Comrade Stalin fought so hard for. But they spit on the earth as they pass me, presumably to propitiate their fecund God in my presence. I cannot understand why communism does not bring them prosperity, as it has done for the Russian peasants. Marxism is scientific, it is something that can be used on anyone. These people simply refuse to learn, of that I am sure.

I want to pity them but they hate me. They do nothing for themselves, so they blame us for their failures. The country is rich and fruitful, with great reserves of coal and iron ore, but they have never developed it. They built no dams or roads or power stations, no highways or schools. All this work has been done by the Soviet government. What is worse is that they seem to have no desire to progress. The only buildings worth noting are the churches, and it seems their troublesome God inhabits certain trees, which then cannot be felled. So far I have accommodated them in this respect. They refuse to master nature: one boy even tried to tell me that nature itself can take revenge. In fact, it was this boy who Vanya prevented from being drafted into the Red Army. His father has gone to Siberia, and now his mother needs someone to care for her. I suppose it is fair enough. Unlike most of the others, she has only three children.

Oh, it's difficult, mama. I want so many things. Just someone to talk to, someone other than a drunken husband and

stupid, idolatrous peasants. I want to come home. But I still
think I am needed here, so a new world can be built on the
ruins of the old. Sometimes I feel that I can't go on, but I
know that I must. Please remember me on May Day, and think
of the great future!

IT WAS true. Kommissar Vanya went to the Party headquarters
in Khmel'nik to arrange for Vitaly's exemption from conscription into the Red Army. Comrade Vanya knew that conscription was erratic and partial: sometimes every male between
eighteen and thirty in a given kolkhoz would be called up,
sometimes the Red Angel would pass over the rooftops, and
no one would be taken. Even so, Vanya wanted to prepare
for any eventuality, so he went into Khmel'nik, into the offices
of NKVD Comrade Zhivkov. At the reception desk, he felt
small and frightened. Zhivkov's secretary had difficulty
believing he was a real collective farm kommissar, until he
showed his papers. He was very careful not to use any
Ukrainian words, but his accent gave him away. It did not
surprise him that the time of his appointment soon passed,
that he was left alone in the waiting room and seen to last.

Vanya and Judit had seen Natasha Kovalenko pushing the
plough. Vitaly stood in for the horse, pulling. It was raining.
The rain flowed in rivulets down the faces of the mother and
the boy. The mud sucked at their feet, holding them in the
one place. Finally, Vitaly slipped over and the plough fell on
him. He pushed the implement away and struggled upright,
his chest and face caked with black mud. Judit hung her head.

'Comrade Stalin did not say it would be like this.'

'No, he did not; he did not.'

'Can we help them?'

Vanya looked into Vitaly's face, trying to engage his vision.
Vitaly stared into the dull, gunmetal-grey distance. Vanya

could see nothing in his eyes. Nothing. 'I will try, dear Judit. I will try.'

Comrade Zhivkov signed Vitaly's release papers, whistling under his breath. He said, 'For once, Comrade Ivan Bohdanovich, you do not smell like a distillery. This is truly a good thing for Kolkhoz 28.'

KATERYNA: When the communists decided who to take to the school for Komsomol students, they felt that the harvest was more important than education, so, as I told you earlier, only a few of us went. We didn't want to leave, and my brother Evheny later ran away from school. When the four of us— there were only four—left on the train for the school, which was near Kiev, the communists let some of the people from the collective and from Khmel'nik come to see us off. My mother came with Vitaly, and Kolya Manchuk stood on the platform with his wife and baby daughter. He was just nine-teen, and already married and a father. The kommissar and his doctor wife were there too—she had to hold him up because he was drunk already, even though it was only 8 a.m.

My mother's face was a painting. She had waxy skin, big, widely spaced green eyes, and was still wearing a scarf over her head, over her thin brown hair. Only thirty-six, and already old. Evheny's face was a photograph, more modern, with wavy, taffy-coloured hair like mother's was once, and crinkled evenly above his ears. Eyes like emeralds, angry, spitting. I did not appreciate *how* angry.

My mother gathered the scarf with knobbly, arthritic hands at her throat, while she was flanked on either side by Nikolai and Vitaly. Vitaly's hair was blond and golden, his eyes big and wide and honest, and blue. Hate and cornflowers. Later the Germans were to praise his pretty face, and the Polish girls in Treblinka village would look after him with lustful expressions on their faces. Nikolai was short compared to my brother, with great wide shoulders and a carefully cultivated moustache. His wife was little and fair, and tired. Her eyes were delineated by old, yellow bruises and her jawline was marked with a faint line of purple. She burped the child over her back, and smiled thinly. Kolya tried to be a good husband, but he had no hope, even less than his wife, and he beat her. The grey-headed kommissar walked away and sat on the platform bench, his head drooping. I looked carefully at his hard wife. You killed my brother. We'll get you, you know. Her husband let his head hang towards the concrete pavement.

At the school, the children of kommissars all over the Ukraine were in attendance. They had nicer uniforms and real socks that stayed up. We Ukrainians bound our feet with *onuchi*, which are like long strips of cloth, instead of using socks. Their winter clothes never had holes in them, or the telltale thinning that foreshadows a hole. They had nice, yellow sweaters, soft and fluffy, the colour of lemon-drops. Often they were Jewish and Russian, and they formed 'non-Ukrainian' cliques, staying away from us. They did not like it when we bested them in schoolwork, or when we talked to the Ukrainian Red Army guards in the school, and they had trouble understanding what we said. But at least we were fed, even though the gruel they gave us was full of weevils. I remember eating the weevils. They tasted a bit like mint.

Once a group of us beat one of them up and stole her sweater, but then there was a huge fight over who got to keep it, so we gave it to Shura the Kalmyk, who liked us all. He helped us forget that it was barbed wire and armed guards that kept us at our studies. Shura kept the sweater for 'a poor girl who might need it'.

It was at this time that the communists told us about the 'disappeared' villages. I saw one with my cadre when I was sixteen. There were shells of burnt-out huts, a pathetic crooked sign outside which read 'Drohobyk' still, and old bones mouldering in the dirt thereabouts. Some of the oldest students were taken to a communist prison in Kiev. People heard from these students that the guards and the kommissars were Jewish and Russian, and that the prisoners were all Ukrainian, with gouged-out eyes, so that they could not see to escape.

Not long after this, when I had been at the school three and a half years, the communists began to tell us what a good fellow Hitler was, and there were lots of posters of Hitler and Stalin shaking hands plastered all over the school. We were taught the Nazi salute. 'The salute of the Ancient Romans', the teachers told us. This was the time of the non-aggression pact, and Shura was disappointed with the Germans. He shook his head when he came to greet us in the mornings, and sighed. Shortly afterwards, he was mobilised and sent to Litovsk, and the school kommissar called everyone to assembly.

'Today, momentous things have happened. With our German friends, we have reclaimed the territory once held by the wicked tsars, and can now bring about a workers' revolution in Poland!' Initially we thought that the Soviet Union had conquered all of Poland, but then he told us it was 'only half.' He stood up on his tippy-toes and yelled that 'we must celebrate this great day with Comrades Hitler and Stalin! Let us sing!' We sang the 'Internationale', and even though we thought that the song was a load of rubbish, Ukrainians are fond of singing (and it is generally recognised that we sing well and pleasingly) so we sang with gusto. The cadre leader who had beaten me three years before sat on the stage in a leather chair, her face in raptures. The Ukrainian cattle did not sing like cows, which was some consolation, and she smiled.

In class we were given information about Poland. The Poles had been wicked fascists. Marshal Piłsudski, their former leader, had persecuted the Jews. He was wicked. Some people thought that maybe Marshal Piłsudski wasn't so bad, for a

Pole. Then we were told that he had also persecuted the Ukrainians in the Polish-owned city of L'vóv. Perhaps the communists were telling lies. No one could be sure. 'The Polish fascists are Roman Catholic,' the Jewess from Leningrad said. 'They all have to do what the Pope tells them. The women all have to have lots of children, whether they want to or not. The Pope tells them to do this.' The Soviet Union— that was us—had to free the poor workers and the poor women from the Roman Catholic Church. I remember thinking *aren't the workers and women Catholic too? Maybe they don't want to be liberated.* The Jewess from Leningrad was clever enough to anticipate my silent question. She leaned forward in her chair, wriggling her fingers expressively.

'The women and the workers, they want to be free of the church. The church keeps them enslaved to capitalism. God was supposed to be on Marshal Piłsudski's side, and yet he lost against our workers' army, remember. We Marxists want to free the Polish people from the shackles of the church and the Pope, just as you have been freed, and just as I have been freed.'

The Pope seemed bad, but Marx was worse. The Pope was alive. Marx issued orders from the grave.

Then she told us how her parents in the Tsarist days were not allowed to leave the *shtetl* because they were Jewish, and how drunken murderous Cossacks would come and disrupt market days and weddings each Easter, because they blamed the Jews for the death of Christ. This was why communism had liberated her. It was too late for her parents, but at least she was able to experience the workers' paradise. It was a sad story, and when she first related it, we all felt sorry for her family: but because she had told it so many times, and was such a nasty person, people slowly lost this feeling. The Jewess from Leningrad did not see the starvation and slaughter in the villages and in the fields. She chose not to see it.

One of the students later asked if Comrade Hitler believed in God. 'No,' she said. 'He believes in his German heritage, and in the strength of the German people, just as Comrade Stalin believes in the strength of the Russian people, so that we can build socialism in one country. After all, we are all Russians together.'

SHURA stands before Kateryna, his narrow eyes leaking tears. Asian people *leak* she thinks. Tears tip over their fleshy lower eyelids, squirting a good way down their faces before coming to rest on their chins. The tears of white people do not travel half as far.

'Soon I am going to Brest-Litovsk,' he says. 'I am not sure when they are taking me. I will never see you again. That is too bad. Here. Have this sweater. You may need it.' He steps forward, and they hug, gently. They are standing on the straw-covered floor of the Young Pioneers equipment shed. It is full of blankets and uniforms and old copies of *Pravda*. It smells faintly of newsprint and rags. She can feel his supple fingers undoing the buttons of her blouse, and does not resist. She has not felt affection since coming to the school, and does not care that she will be *ruined*. Yes. *Ruined*. That's what her mother says. 'That's why Nikolai and Lara were married so suddenly. She. . .she. . .she got herself ruined.' 'My mother says you're ruined,' she had nearly said to Lara Manchuk one bright winter's day. She slides her long arms around his warm, bare back under his uniform, waiting while he unbuttons his top. One-handed, he spreads it on the straw, and they sit together, quietly. She curls up beside him, her head on his chest; she can see him holding his erect penis in one hand and reaches out to touch it with her fingers. He is whispering in her hair, and his tears are making her shoulders wet and salty. She does not feel anything in particular when he is inside her, but she does not want him to leave.

The next day, trucks arrive to take all the soldiers in the school to Brest-Litovsk. It is early—only 0500 hours—but she hears the heavy diesels heading down the long drive lined with fir trees. She looks out of the small barred window and waves, but she does not see him. Only a multitude of caps and stars.

KATERYNA: A few months later, we began to receive Ukrainian students from L'vóv and Tarnopol, cities in Polish West Ukraine. They could already read and write, and some of them spoke Polish as well as Ukrainian. They hated communism, and made no secret of it, coming from fascist Poland. They believed in God, wore Orthodox and Catholic crosses on their necks and wrists and said prayers at night. They came from real families, where people owned houses and land and dairy cattle—even poor people. They resented being removed from their homes and schools and churches, which the communists burnt down. But even in Polish West Ukraine, things were not so simple or so sweet. There had never been starvation there, but the Piłsudski regime made sure that the Ukrainian-language schools in the district were underfunded, and closed Ukrainian-language newspapers. They also told us that this was minor compared to the doings of the Bolsheviks.

They had horror stories about deportations and conscription. They were officially designated as 'orphans', but their parents were still alive, somewhere in Siberia. They prayed to God, and hoped for revenge. The priests had educated them, and despite the best efforts of the communists, the priests owned them.

The Jewess from Leningrad forced them to give up their religious jewellery one morning in assembly, and it made quite a significant pile on the floor beneath the podium, which was decorated with the communist flag. They walked out to the middle of the floor with such dignity: singly, bracelet and crucifix and charm in hand. Even the kommissar was shamed. He refused to look at them as they approached. Instead, he

31

buried his head in his hands, and stared at the top of his desk through his fingers. Finally, they gathered at the far end of the hall and started to sing 'Te Deum'. They had managed only a few bars when some members of the school's NKVD garrison chased them, still singing, from the building.

They knew everything, it seemed, and at night, after lights out, they would tell us what they knew. One big boy, nearly eighteen, Ivan from L'vóv, hopped down from his bunk at midnight, when the cadre leaders had gone to bed.

'Hey, you know what the stinking Jews did to Petlyura?' His round face was filled with light. None of us even knew that Petlyura was dead. I knew that he had been exiled by the Bolsheviks to France, and I was sure that this was common knowledge. Only later did I realise that most people knew nothing, and thus simply believed the students from Polish West Ukraine. We listened in awed silence. We knew so little.

Ivan licked his lips. 'They hired an assassin and sent him to Paris, where Petlyura was exiled by the Bolsheviks.'

'Where's Paris?' asked a young, uneducated voice.

'It's the capital of France, idiot.'

'Where's France?'

'Aaarghh. It's on the other side of Germany.'

'Ohhh.'

'They hired this assassin, in 1926, anyway. His name was Shalom Schwarzbard. Before he went out and killed Petlyura in cold blood, he wrote to his wife. You know what he wrote?' Ivan inclined his face upwards, and held his hands before him like a praying Jew, intoning the words in a nasal, whining monotone.

'He wrote "I am performing a duty for our poor people. I am going to avenge all the pogroms, all the blood." Then he went right out, on the 26th of May, and shot Petlyura in the head. Seven bullets, all calculated and planned. He'd been watching Petlyura for days, so he knew when he was home.

And he was under instructions from Moscow. Moscow wanted Petlyura out of the way.'

'Shame.'

'Terrible shame.'

'But Hitler's being really friendly with the Bolshies now. I thought we might get our country back.'

Other voices agreed. 'What are we going to do now? You can't trust the Germans either. Hitler and Stalin are "comrades" now.'

Ivan shook his head. 'I don't know,' he said. 'Maybe Hitler is waiting for the right moment. Maybe he truly is an evil man. Maybe we have to wait. For a long time.'

The girls' quarters were separated from the boys', and we crowded around the doorway to their dorm, listening, watching for cadre leaders and teachers, whispering and giggling. Ivan wanted us to come in, but he didn't know that we would all be beaten if caught in the boys' quarters at 0100 hours, so we loitered outside.

'We'll have our country,' he continued. 'I'm sure of that. But it may take many years.'

Ivan was taken away for the Red Army. The others were beaten into silence, but they were confident that changes would come. One boy the NKVD kept awake for a week with water torture and beatings. He had a list of all the kommissars and cadre leaders in the school. He and several other students killed most of them in Kiev soon after the Germans captured the city.

TWO

It was tough to control but, oh, it was a nice feeling—all the bullets coming out. I was thinking it would be nice to have some Serbs standing in front of me.

Goran Ivanisevic, after telling reporters that friends had taught him how to fire a machine-gun, 1993

My family migrated to Australia in the early 1950s. Vitaly was the first to come, leaving the DP camp in Stuttgart in 1948. He worked on the Snowy Mountains Hydro-Electric Scheme for some time, then purchased a strawberry and flower farm in Brisbane in the days when Brisbane was more rural than urban. When he finally had to sell the farm, a Big W shopping centre was built on the site. 'Just another stage in the concreting-over of Australia,' he said. He worked at that farm, 'did well' at it. I remember visiting it, playing among tumbling wisteria and bougainvillea. Finishing up covered over with scratches and red soil, then waiting under the porch while Vitaly served piroshki and orange juice to my brother and me, and piroshki and vodka to the grown-ups. Sometimes we would be allowed to pick strawberries for an afternoon. 'Two in the mouth, one in the bag,' Vitaly would tease.

He waited until he was forty to marry again. He had been married in the war, but the topic was taboo. He married Staciya. No one seemed to know how he met her. Staciya was another Ukrainian immigrant, a childless widow ten years older than Vitaly. She dressed in old-fashioned headscarves, and brought pictures of her parents and her home town into the house. The home-town picture was old and tinted, green, with low hills, and a sky that must have once been iridescent blue. They 'grew old' together, like the line in the Browning poem says, came each year to my school's speech night, were proud and pleased when I won academic prizes or was made editor of the school magazine.

My father would talk in the old language to Vitaly and Staciya, making my mother feel terribly left out. 'I suppose I should start speaking in Gaelic,' she said crossly on more than one occasion. 'See how they manage then.' My father migrated to Australia in 1950, along with my mother. They met in England, where he had been a European Voluntary Worker, imported to work on a dairy farm. Unlike Vitaly, Evheny Kovalenko had been to school. He wanted to make something of his life. He promised Maggie Collins that he would always look after her.

They settled in Cairns. He cut cane, he sold insurance, cars and fridges, and was unemployed twice, before finally landing a good job as a clerk in an engineering firm. He tried to join the Chamber of Commerce, but they told him that they 'didn't want any Balt bastards and women in the Chamber of Commerce'. Maggie had five children, and they sent these five children to a good school and made sure that they matriculated at the top of their classes. The school academic honour board had five Kovalenkos on it. I was the late afterthought, the 'family surprise', as dad called it. The school must have been appalled when another of us appeared. Once again they had to put up with this loud, chatty, migrant family with excessively ambitious children.

My father loved my mother dearly, and I admired him for this. Other kids' parents were always fighting. My parents started to fight and then would finish up collapsing with laughter. Schoolfriends who stayed over said it was like being on the set for 'Fawlty Towers' for hours at a time. My dad was even as tall as John Cleese.

We would talk amongst ourselves after the academic prizes had been awarded. We would laugh at the local politician or businessman who had presented the prizes, who had found our surname difficult to pronounce, who had stood shaking my hand for far too long while struggling with those awful syllables. Sometimes my aunt was there, my beautiful aunt Kateryna from Western Australia. Her husband Cliff MacDermot was a big amiable Scot who had once played professional Australian Rules Football. He raised her two wartime children with her, my 'big cousins', Bernie and Anton. Aunt Kateryna came to Australia in 1951, as a 'family migrant'. She also came through England, and she met Cliff on the boat on the way over. Mum said that the story of this meeting and marriage was the 'Kovalenko contribution to Mills & Boon romance'. Kateryna had a third child by Cliff; this girl was youngish, like my oldest brother, Bret. Cliff said she was 'a sort of radical'. She got herself arrested in protest marches. Siobhan MacDermot did her own thing; she did not always come to our family gatherings. She was a 'roaring feminist', also according to Cliff. She liked us, but thought we were 'terribly unfashionable'. Kateryna had been married before, like Vitaly. The subject was more than taboo. The mere mention of it meant a smack on the arse and expulsion from the house. Bernie and Anton knew who their father was, and where he was now. I was not allowed to know about Kateryna's family history, except that it was 'tragic'. My brother John was not allowed to know either. But he was eight years older than me. They had to tell him eventually. My biggest brother, Bret, he knew. So did my biggest sister, Natalya. And they also knew about Dad and uncle Vitaly. John and I wanted to know, but as the years passed, my father grew timid and we grew forgetful.

For my benefit, my parents moved to Brisbane, close to the school my brothers and sisters had attended as boarders. This is where I remember Vitaly best, growing old on his farm, coming to school speech nights, talking with the family, my father, my mother. Mum and Cliff could almost understand each other's Gaelic. Vitaly and Staciya and Kateryna would talk quickly and enthusiastically in Ukrainian, Cliff would laugh kindly at their waving arms. My father would doze on the grass in front of Vitaly's porch, hands and legs crossed and glasses askew, sometimes mumbling interjections. Then Mum would get cross, and English would be spoken for the rest of the night. My funny old family, clucking and chattering in a language that I did not wish to speak. I understood them, but I would always answer in English.

MOTHER caught me looking at the photographs, spread all over the coverlet. 'Oh! The Lord above! The child's found those infernal pictures!' Dad was carting groceries up the front steps. I heard her agitated conversation with him. My father said nothing—nothing that I could hear. He trudged into the bedroom, a head of celery tucked under his arm. Mother had her head in her hands. 'You should have burnt those bloody things, Evheny. I've been saying that for years!' I gathered the photographs into a neat pile, and handed them to my father. 'Sorry, Dad,' I cried. 'I was looking for the Rubik's cube.' He took them from me, gently. He was also crying. I could see big tears rolling down his cheeks.

'You know about World War Two?' my mother asked.
'Yes, Mum.'

'You know that the English and Australians and the Americans fought against the Germans?'

'Yes, Mum.'

'Well, dad was on the German side.'

'But we're not German!'

'Hush. And my father is not English, but he helped the English.'

'But it's all right if you were on the other side. Drew Gunter at school, his grandad was in the German army in the war. . .he brought his grandad's helmet to school for show and tell. It was really neat. It had a swastika on the side of it. Miss Wilston said that the Germans were just as brave as the Aussies except that they lost.'

My father looked at me, shaking his head. 'For us, it is different.'

'But if you were just like Drew Gunter's grandad. . .'

'If anyone asks, you may tell them that I was on the German side, but you cannot say anything else.'

'Like Drew Gunter's grandad?'

'Yes.'

'Have you got any groovy things, like a helmet?'

'Don't be silly. But yes, I do. Some nice enamel pins, and a medal.'

'Will you tell me what happened really, one day?'

'One day.'

SO THIS is a trip into the past, I remind myself as I pass Dreamworld. I take the Hope Island turn-off. Hope Island. Famous for Sanctuary Cove, the 'Ultimate Resort'. The place where they tell us that 'not all the animals are in the zoo'. I pass a new golf course. It resembles a ploughed paddock. Japanese tourists clamber over the freshly laid turf. In the distance, a new and ugly clubhouse gleams. Vitaly and Staciya live in the old section of the island; they moved here before

Hope Island became 'touristy'. I turn into Vitaly's driveway. I notice that the banksia in his front yard has finally been coaxed into producing its fragrant yellow brush-flowers.

I looked at the pins. Once, soon after my terrible discovery. An enamel badge showing a blue and yellow flag. A fancy, winged eagle clutching a swastika in its claws. A cloth patch with a silver skull and crossbones on it. The idea developed in my head that Daddy had been a pirate. Pirates were bad. They were also glamorous.

But the photographs and the pretty pins lingered guiltily in my mind. For years I was unable to watch war movies without suppressing a bleak shudder. Documentary items about the Holocaust made me feel queasy and faint. When I was cast as Anne Frank in the school play I declined the role, then went home and threw up.

I walk up the long drive.

'Was that true about you hiding under the kitchen table?'

He is rummaging in the kitchen cupboard. 'Tea or Coffee?'

'Tea. I fancy a cuppa.'

'Yes, it's true. I don't know why I did it.'

'What?'

'Why I hide under the bloody table.' He is irritated, I can tell. He appears behind the kitchen bench. His white hair hangs over his face as he concentrates on making the tea. He smiles at last, and his eyes disappear behind crinkles of skin. Blue eyes. Beautiful blue eyes. He pulls his round bifocals out of his pocket. 'It's a mongrel being old,' he grumbles. 'Can't bloody see.' He pushes the glasses sharply at his face.

'Where's Staciya?' I ask.

'Doctor. She had to get more of those little green pills. She's sick all the time. No dog for her to walk anymore.'

I remember his old cattle dog, on the farm. The dog that he called 'Bohdan' but that everyone else called 'Blue'. The dog answered to both names, would gleefully chase tennis balls struck in childish cricket tests, even when he was fifteen years old. He died last winter.

'Found a replacement for Blue, then?' I ask.

'Bohdan? Never. Best dog in the world, that dog.' He looks up, seriously, eyes blazing. He stares at me, the animus located in his eyes alone.

'Do you think they'll put me on trial? In South Australia?'

'I don't know. They have to find enough information about you for a trial. Otherwise, the charges will be dropped.'

'Will I have to go to gaol? What about Staciya? She's old, older than me.' He sits down, hangs his head over his tea. 'I'm scared, Fiona. Not for me, but for Staciya, and for you and Maggie and everyone. Imagine the shame of having an uncle in gaol. Terrible shame!'

'They'll only send you to gaol if they find you guilty. And they can only find you guilty if they try you. The trial may not even happen.' I want to reach out and touch his hand, but I cannot. I want to say that there is no shame, but that would be a lie. He stirs his tea, gently.

'It would be very hard to convict you. And we have no extradition treaty with Israel, so they can't send you there, either.'

'Extradition treaty? What's that?'

'It's an agreement between governments to allow for the removal of people charged with crimes from one country to another so they can be put on trial. We don't have one with Israel. America has one with Israel, that's why John Demjanjuk is on trial there.'

'I knew Ivan the Terrible,' he says softly. 'Not very well, but I knew him. The one they have in Israel isn't him. He's too short. The real Ivan the Terrible was a giant, much bigger than me.' He sips his tea. I walk outside, kicking at the sandy soil. His yard is a mess, with tractor parts and piles of topsoil scattered all around it. His clothes line is suspended on wire loops nailed to the wall, because the pole has rusted. His TV antenna is a weird contraption held up with putty and brads. He's too stingy to buy a new one, so he tries to pick up SBS with an antenna that looks like something rescued from the town dump.

I wonder if he has remembered to take his diuretic pills since the trials started. His face is red, the veins on his neck stand out. When he went to the naturopath last August, she leaned across her desk and said 'Your liver has the right to take you to court and sue you for every other vital organ in your system.' She prescribed cod liver oil, and twelve glasses of water a day, and 'definitely no more vodka, Mr Kovalenko.' I hope he has been going to his AA meetings, taking his tablets, drinking his water. I wish all these things for him.

He yells at me through the ragged screen. 'You going to let your tea go cold?' I push the frail door aside, let it click behind me. 'Kateryna says she has been talking to you.' I nod.

'I sent her some tapes to record herself,' I say, 'to save marathon STD calls to Perth. I sent her five 90-minute tapes, and she filled the lot, both sides. I thought about transcribing it all, but it's taking ages. Some of it's in Ukrainian, as well. I don't know. I should keep it, record it. But it's hard to own things when they're bad. To admit that they belong to you.'

I gaze into my tea. I am losing my coherence. I struggle on. 'And some of the things she says, you know. . .I think that well. . .I mean, I never thought my aunt had thoughts like that. My aunt. And the German she married. God. Like some serial killer, a loony, a nutter. You know.' Vitaly looks at me, kindly.

'You don't understand, but that's all right. In those days, people didn't say no, or start protesting. We were too scared. Both Germans and Russians, they were very. . .strong. We just did what we were told. Kateryna too.'

'But you didn't have to volunteer! You could have run away! If you could go back, would you join the SS or go to Finland?'

'Oh, Fiona,' he says, staring down at the slate tiles, 'people didn't have choices like that.' He takes off the handsome gold-framed spectacles I have always admired. 'It's terrible. Even these once belonged to a Jew.'

THE INVASION of the Soviet Union had a grim structure to it, a ballet where the dancers knew their steps, but not the whole routine. German planes screeched in formation above the schools and cities and collectives of the Ukraine. Russian soldiers burned crops as they beat a hasty retreat, and they frequently encountered angry, armed peasants who refused to give up their produce so easily. In one village, a soldier with a flamethrower was hit on the back of the head with a shovel wielded by a seventy-year-old woman, who calmly returned to her house amid the screeching of Stukas and the dull thump of artillery. In another, despite the sounding of sirens, people sat on their roofs to watch the pretty dogfights above, pointing out which plane was Russian or German to their children. The aurora borealis came over the collectives in the Ukraine, and all the different lights danced and jumped together, both natural and man-made.

Nikolai Manchuk was shouting, shouting; he ran along the streets of the village, then into the fields. 'Come up from the fields, father! The Russians are going! The Russians are going!' The green and pink light exploded and slipped through the sky above him, and he waved his arms, his face turning first green, then purple and orange and pink. Stukas flew beneath the northern lights, screaming. Groups of children stood in the fields, the wheat above their heads, staring up at the sky, their parents gathered in dumb silence beside them. In the village, the kommissar was arrested and tied to the leg of his kitchen table, and a search party was sent out after his wife, who had disappeared along with the Red Army. A dozen Red Army Ukrainians who had gone A.W.O.L in the confusion of the invasion turned up in the main street and began hunting for communists and Jews, while the village settled down to wait for the Germans.

Vitaly had been given a rifle by one of the soldiers, and he now sat pensively guarding the kommissar, on the front steps, his back propped against the door frame, waiting for dawn.

Vanya's wrists were tied together behind him and to the table leg. His legs stuck out in front, awkwardly, slightly bent at the knees. His breathing came in short gasps, because someone had kicked him in the stomach, and he pleaded incessantly.

'Vitaly? Vitaly. . .are you listening to me?'

Vitaly swivelled around, levelling his rifle. 'Shut the fuck up, communist. You're only staying alive until the Germans get here, and then we're going to string you up.'

'Vitaly, I let your brother stay away from the school, doesn't that count? I'm sorry about your woman, but my wife stood in my way. . .I stopped you from being conscripted, so you could help your mother. . . you didn't know that, did you? I don't hate you, Vitaly. Don't punish me. Please.' Wheedle. Bargain. Smile. The boy's face was marked with angry splendour.

'You couldn't do anything to save Hryhory Manchuk. Kolya had to find his own uncle with his balls and nose and eyes all hacked off, just because of a tractor.'

'But Vitaly, we used to have happy times—reading stories up here.'

Vitaly did not listen. He had nothing else to say. He didn't really hate the kommissar, but it felt good all the same. He looked over the gun-sight, his fingers white with the exertion of holding the rifle in the same position.

Vanya rolled sickeningly to one side, his face streaked with tears. 'Don't kill me Vitaly. Please don't kill me. I'm one of yours.' He looked up, briefly. The boy still had the rifle levelled at his heart, his young, serious face concentrated with effort. 'How old are you, Vitaly?'

'Nineteen. Twenty in October.'

'What are you going to do with your young life, Vitaly?'

'I'm going to fight against the Bolsheviks for a free Ukraine.'

The accumulated hatred of all the years exploded now. Gleefully people tore down pictures of Lenin and Stalin, and more particularly, Marx. The big glossy images of the bearded philosopher were laid out in the streets and pissed on by men and women. Sometimes the defecting Red Army soldiers who appeared in the villages and towns would round up Jews and communists and make them lie on the pissy posters and then would play Russian roulette with them. The villagers felt certain of their imminent liberation.

Nikolai Manchuk stole the kommissar's flat-bed truck and drove into the nearby town of Khmel'nik with Evheny, where he exchanged a quantity of valuables taken from some of the Jews for a truckload of vodka. Spectacular scenes of rejoicing were enacted in Khmel'nik, where people danced and cried. A lot of Red Army soldiers were performing fancy Cossack steps in the streets, and Nikolai assumed they were Cossacks who had decided enough was enough and had taken the opportunity to change sides. They stared at him and ogled the truck, thinking it was his. They were so drunk that they did not see the hammer and sickle painted on the driver's door, and could not hear the crash of the gears as Nikolai learned to drive as he sped along.

Later, on foot, he met a drunken priest with robes awry who kept babbling about the Fourth Horseman, and he let Evheny dance briefly with some of the Cossacks. He vaguely remembered the priest from the village. A little worldly vodka priest without courage. One of the Cossacks had heard that the Germans were in Vinnitsa already, and would be coming back around in a big circle, but he wasn't sure. Evheny was worried about his sister, in a Communist Party school near Kiev, and Nikolai gave him vodka to calm him down. The two of them returned to the village after three in the morning, deeply sozzled, to find the celebrations had gained momentum. Nikolai distributed the vodka from the cab of the truck to eager patrons while Evheny found his brother and mother. Women had baked loaf upon loaf of delicious bread to welcome the Germans; their children sat at their feet, playing in the powdery dust.

At seven o'clock in the morning, when the village was shimmering in the beautiful golden pink light of morning in late summer, one hundred and seventeen German soldiers marched into the main street, to be greeted with gifts of bread and salt by its happy, drunken inhabitants. To the great joy of the locals, many of these Germans spoke Ukrainian, and were in fact members of the Ukrainian 'Nachtigall' battalion, formed by the Nazis in Polish West Ukraine. Already drunk from celebrations earlier in the morning in Khmel'nik, this group, along with a few others, had been sent on by their commanding officers to occupy the neighbouring villages. They gave the children chocolate and sweets, and milled around with the locals, taking happy snaps to send home to relatives in Poland and Germany; they gathered at Nikolai's temporary bar and proceeded to join in the alcoholic celebrations. By mid-afternoon, the village slept under a warm, boozy haze. Bodies lay prostrate in the street, across door-jambs, leaned up against walls. Someone had thought to give the kommissar enough vodka to send him off as well, and he lay crumpled underneath his kitchen table, snoring noisily, his wrists still tied both together and to the table leg.

The Germans from the Reich itself were exotic, like imported butterflies, and their fair, pink skin was considered fascinating. As a result of this interest, a few Wehrmacht and Ukrainian women satisfied themselves with great energy upstairs in the kommissar's house. They made a racket, but otherwise the village was silent.

THE LITTLE priest is glad he can wear his robes again, so long in mothballs, hidden below the stairs. He incites the town against the Jews and communists, because it is easy to feel the glib assurances pour from his lips. He is not even asking

46

for grim mortification without knowing the pain involved, as he had done in the Good Old Days. Already drunk, the people of Khmel'nik take him at his word, and hunt for their enemies with pitchforks and scythes.

The priest does not feel very brave. He did not become one of the holy martyrs. When the communists issued their anti-clerical laws, he renounced his celibacy and married. . .well, not what the Church would call married, but you know. She is a good woman. He sits on the church steps. He is as drunk as his parishioners; vaguely he sees the wives of dead communists dragged through the streets to be raped behind what was once his church.

One of the Cossack rapists staggers towards him and begs for absolution, a vinous light in his eyes. 'It was drink! The drink! Our Father who art in Heaven Hail Mary full of grace oh I don't remember, Father.' The priest shuts his eyes. The Cossack's hands are curled into claws. He is kneeling. There are clean patches on his grimy cheeks where the tears have flowed. He is kissing the ring on the priest's hand. The priest sees that he has fashioned the red star on his cap into a Christian cross. 'My son,' he says, 'it is not mine to give. I am a vodka priest. I violate God's commandments every day. Even though I have the holy task of transforming the bread and wine into God's body. I am married.' The Cossack gesticulates wildly. 'Our priest! Our priest! Ha ha. Our priest is married!' He pours vodka over the priest's head and follows a group of Ukrainian women up the street. The women are hitting something with pitchforks and shovels. The priest squints at their blurred body movements. An NKVD man, one of the ones who did not run away with his comrades, is at the centre of the melee; his head is a bloody ball.

In the town's houses, in the hearths where these women ruled, his faith was kept alive for him. In books smuggled in each month from L'vóv, mothers would read to their children about the holy martyrs, and how Satan was getting ready to

47

assault poor Ukraine. How Stalin and his Jewish friends drafted the anti-clerical laws. How Stalin/Satan lined all the priests up against a wall. How the priests always died shouting 'Khristos Voskrese'. But the children were not allowed to ask 'what about Father Pyotr? Is he not a priest?' 'Don't even mention that name to me,' the mothers would answer. 'He is lower than worms and maggots.'

Someone finally kills the kommissar, but he is too drunk to notice his own death. His wife is found hiding three kilometres away in a roadside ditch full of water, by two defecting Red Army Tartars. They laugh at her in a way that sounds good-natured, and help her climb out of the ditch. Assuming their Red Army uniforms to be signifiers of belief in the Soviet State, she tells them that she loves only Comrade Stalin and the Soviet Union. They grimace with hate. One of them yells 'Bolshie!' and lunges at her. She is raped, and left partly clad on the road shoulder, alive. The massacre is terrible, terrible. But in the boozy haze of the morning, no one notices.

KATERYNA: When the Germans invaded, plans were drafted to evacuate our school to Kiev, forty kilometres away, and we joined the great stream of refugees heading east. Thousands of people, ragged and dispirited, marched between fields of burning crops, pushed onwards by cadre leaders and NKVD troops. At night, the whole Ukraine seemed to be alight, as the Red Army burnt the unharvested crop. German planes strafed the straggling columns, and when people ran to take refuge in nearby stands of conifers, the Stukas dropped a chemical onto the trees that made them explode into flame.

Pitched battles erupted between NKVD troops and the Ukrainian and Cossack units of the Red Army. The NKVD used the refugees as shields, and bodies were strewn all along the main road to Kiev. We were within sight of the city when we learned that the Germans had encircled it in a giant pincer movement—the message was relayed the whole length of the refugee columns. A large group of German soldiers approached our group on horseback, followed by a tank, assisting the Red Army Ukrainians against the NKVD. When the communists saw the enemy coming *from* Kiev, they surrendered, only to be pushed off the road by the Germans and Ukrainians and shot. Some of the refugees cheered at this, but those who had been burnt in the forest sat in the roadway, wailing, their cries mingling with the bursts of machine-gun fire.

The tank and several Germans moved on to fight the last of the NKVD behind us, while German medics laid the injured refugees on stretchers and tried to treat their wounds. Through the seated groups of refugees, one could see the orderlies bandaging burns and chasing away flies, themselves grimy with smoke and dust. Behind them, the NKVD were lined up and shot more neatly, in groups, as they were marched forward by their captors. A tall, fair-skinned man in black directed them to where they should stand.

I watched as two Germans laid one of the students from our school on a stretcher. The girl was badly burnt: she howled with pain, and I could see the more senior of the two Germans stroking her hair back from her eyes while the younger man dressed her burns. The tall man was still shouting orders to his newly acquired Ukrainians, jabbing with his fingers. 'Not like that, like this. Shoot here. Then you don't waste bullets.' I looked around. The Jewish cadre leader from Leningrad sat in the dirt not two metres from me, an expression of raw fear on her face. She watched as the Germans shot and ministered; when she saw me she made a tiny, noiseless snarl.

After about fifty of the NKVD had been shot, the fair man waved his arms to stop. He said something to the remainder of the terrified NKVD men, and the majority walked over and joined the Ukrainians who had been content to kill them not five minutes earlier. Three who did not were shot, one of them shouting, 'Long live Comrade Stalin!' as he rolled over in the dirt. One of the tall German's underlings passed him a megaphone, and he stood on top of the pile of bodies that his troops had made.

'All right, listen. My name is Wilhelm Hasse. We are going to continue to the city of Kiev, since we're almost there, where you will be housed in temporary accommodation. That is the best we can do. Where is everyone from?' He looked at our group, a concerned expression on his face. 'You kids must be from a school? Where?'

'Near here. We haven't come very far. But I come from Khmel'nik,' I was shouting, and I tried to stand up, brushing the dirt from my skirt. He strolled towards us, flanked by two soldiers with machine-guns. His Ukrainian was clear, though accented.

'I come from L'vóv,' another student yelled.

'Tarnopol' said another.

He pointed at people singly.

'Vinnitsa'

'Dubno'

'Berdichev'

'What the fuck is going on? Don't you people have families?' He was genuinely astonished. His handsome, tanned face grimaced. 'Here,' he held something out to me. 'Have some chocolate.' He pointed to others. 'You too. Here. . .Kretschmann. Give these poor kids some chocolate.' He looked around at the huge crowd of refugees seated in the sun and shook his head. I looked at him. He was the first boss I had ever seen who swore. An earthy boss. He started to walk away.

'Boss,' I called after him. He turned to face me. 'Boss, the communists take some of us away to Communist Party schools to make us Komsomols. They take us away from our families. I want to go to Khmel'nik, where my family is.' He raised his eyebrows. 'How old are you?'

'Eighteen, Boss.'

'Stand up. You're not a beggar, you're an Aryan. And don't call me "boss". I am not an English imperialist.'

I felt his hands under my armpits and scrambled to my feet, chocolate in hand. 'Go on. Eat it. It tastes nice.'

I broke a piece off and put it in my mouth. I had never eaten chocolate before—I only had Ivan from L'vóv's word that it was delicious. The sweetness surprised me, and I salivated. 'Go on. You can have it all. I have plenty.' He broke off another piece, and put it in my mouth, brushing my lips with his fingers. He turned away from me, shouting into the megaphone. 'Come on. On to Kiev. We will guard you, and try and get you home. Come on!'

The straggling columns continued forward. The burnt and the injured were placed on horse-drawn carts. Hasse mounted his own horse, and motioned towards me. 'Want a ride?' he asked, beaming. I nodded. I had learnt to ride years ago, and had not ridden since being taken away to school. He said, 'You're a very pretty girl. You deserve a ride.' He helped me on in front of him, and I looked down. The cadre leader stumbled along beside us. A Ukrainian stood behind her, his rifle ready, poised at the back of her neck, where the red scarf touched the collar of her blouse. She was unaware of his presence. Hasse shook his head at the Ukrainian. 'Not yet. The time will come.' The Ukrainian nodded, and walked to the fringes of the group, arms swinging. He whistled tunefully to himself. The cadre leader turned in panic, watching him go. She looked at me. Her eyes were full of tears.

I dozed in the arms of Willie Hasse; he had to hold on lest I slid off. My head lolled on his shoulder, and when I opened my eyes I would see his tanned face. I could not see his hair hidden under his helmet, but his eyes were bright and clear, bluer than my brother Vitaly's eyes. He smiled at me, and he

51

took off my red scarf and tied it around my hair. Kretschmann kept making lively comments to him in German, but Hasse was boss, I felt sure. He could tell Kretschmann to shut up anytime he liked. He didn't. He smiled at me, and stroked my face with one finger.

AT THE university in Kiel was a young man who hated people. Not all people, just certain, specific kinds of people. He came from a home that was quite dazzling in its cleanliness, and when the homes of others did not match the yardstick of his own home, he usually restricted the intimacy of any friendship that developed. His father was an upright Lutheran pastor, and the austerity of this severe doctrine was played out in the life of the boy. Once, when he was eight or so, he had sat on his bedroom floor, playing with his penis. It was not particularly masturbatory, this playing, and he sat quietly, 'boinging' it back and forth, like a piece of stiff rubber. His father appeared at the door, suddenly, as he tended to do, a question about school dying on his lips when he saw his son. He beat him and beat him, yelling about the evils of the sin of onanism. The boy's penis shrivelled and wilted, trying to retreat inside him. His father affixed a clothes peg to it, to teach him its worth. God would only save the pure.

At school he did well, and read everything. He liked de Gobineau and Nietzsche, and topped the district in mathematics in the tertiary entrance exam. He enrolled at the university to study engineering. It was here that he discovered his need for cleanliness, and at the same time found the atmosphere at home stifling. His father ranted when he left home, but the young man was quite determined. His father was an effete old shit, he said. His balls were dry, and he couldn't come. The son hated dryness and slow death. He wanted to die quickly and gloriously.

His ancestors—Teutonic Knights and handsome, sturdy

Danes—conspired to make him happy with his appearance. It was easy. He felt that Jews were dark and dirty, the western, civilised veneer of the liberals a tissue-thin facade. At this stage, in third year, he was prepared to wait. He waited for his finals and his University Medal. Waited and enjoyed the company of numerous women who had pursued him throughout his degree. Waited and enjoyed the election result that gave his party absolute power.

As a member of the *Einsatzgruppen* which took part in the invasion of Poland, he worked to overcome his nausea at the sight of dirt and blood. He let Polish peasants carve up Jews with scythes. He ordered a synagogue to be burnt, its congregation trapped inside. He worked especially hard at internalising the political doctrines of his superiors, for he was considered a poor-quality Nazi. It was dirt he disliked. Germs. Bacteria. When he heard his commanding officers' cultivated disdain and hatred for the Jews, he would not join in the conversation, but would sit out on the balcony of the officers' mess, alone, cognac or schnapps in hand, giggling. He felt very little, in fact, and was more an interested party to his own actions than an actual participant. During and after the killings he felt nothing.

When his unit invaded the Soviet Union, taking part in the drive south through the Ukraine, he marvelled at what he considered to be the studied bestiality of its inhabitants. The Poles were just cruel. Stupid and cruel. The Ukrainians had less education than the Poles, but they had *style*. He had been reading a substantial amount of Margaret Mead lately, and observed the savages with a scholarly, anthropological eye. He also had a visiting card printed in Warsaw, including his new rank. *'Hauptsturmführer Hasse B Eng Civ(Hons)'* the card read, and underneath, *'Einsatzgruppe C'*. The card informed the casual reader that Captain Hasse was a specialist in metallurgy—lathes, welding, casting and the like.

In the Russian invasion, he faced real danger for the first

time. He was shot at by NKVD and wounded in the fleshy part of his right upper arm. While injured, he saved the life of a Pole serving in the Wehrmacht. The Pole had stepped on a mine, and his foot, still clad in its boot, had flown high into the air, twirling and swirling with eerie grace. Hasse braved enemy fire to pick up the heavy Pole and carry him over his shoulder to safety behind the front line. For this he was awarded the Iron Cross, Second Class. Later, his helmet was shot off and a bridge was blown up under him, but he emerged relatively unscathed. In the cities of the Ukraine, he was welcomed and marvelled at. One woman wanted a lock of his white blond hair. Two other women took turns to have sex with him in a clean, dry hayloft. One woman said afterwards that it was a bit like being diddled by a preacher, and he hit her and hit her. Hit her hard. And had to use every ounce of the charm God had given him to patch up the rift. He succeeded.

He dropped his standards slightly when it came to the cleanliness he demanded from his sexual partners, and screwed his way at a fairly brisk pace across the occupied territories. He would be considered very responsible now, because he always wore a condom, but it was his sense of cleanliness that prevailed. Slavs were still savages, even when attractive and lusty.

Only one element intruded to spoil Willie's pleasure. Erich Kretschmann. Erich Kretschmann was a true believer, a devoted Nazi, or at least liked to present himself in that light. He could not stomach the fact that his commanding officer had received a German military honour for saving the life of a Slav any more than he could cope with being told to give chocolate to Ukrainian children. He watched Hasse's sexual activities with horror, and tried with little success to stop the men serving under him from indulging in the same manner. He could not understand Hasse's willingness to learn Slavic languages; he maintained a fervent belief in Jewish subhumanity, and was irritated when Hasse slept like an exhausted child after an *Einsatzaktion* while he lay awake, tormented by lurid visions. Now he used his one talent—a knack for employing coarse humour to good effect—to annoy Hasse on the triumphant march to Kiev. Hasse had a beautiful, red-headed Ukrainian schoolgirl saddled in front of him. He fed her chocolate and stroked her unblemished skin with his tapered fingers.

Kretschmann was a walking conscience. His lurid racial suprematism nauseated Hasse almost as much as dirt had once done. He would stare, his hazel eyes yellow with hate. Hasse half expected that he would wake up one morning and see that Kretschmann's pupils had elongated, becoming pointed at the vertices, giving him cat's eyes. He said little that was inflammatory, that Hasse as his superior officer could punish. It is what he did not say. At the time Kretschmann was making boisterous, and seemingly harmless, comments about Hasse's sexual prowess. About liking his Slavic tit young. About cradle-snatching. Hasse didn't pay full attention. He was trying to stop his Ukrainian savages from shooting every Jew and communist in the refugee column, and even the NKVD troops who had been bullied into joining the Ukrainians. Plans could not be upset. Finally, he looked at the smirking Kretschmann. 'Shut up, Kretschmann. All right?'

'Yes, sir.' Kretschmann was quiet. He had to be, now. But his silence was crushing.

Do you want to fight Bolshevism? Do you want a free Ukraine? Come and share in the Great and Historic Mission! Come and help build the New Europe, where all people oppressed by Bolshevism will live free from want! If you wish to join in this great battle, then form a queue in Main Street, and sign some forms we have here. The pay is good and the food is better, and you will be riding horses again, you know! Work for you in Khmel'nik and Vinnitsa! Join forces against Bolshevism! Young men between the ages of eighteen and twenty-five! If you have families, transport will be provided for them! Sign the paper! Sign the paper! Sign the paper here!

'They won't let you in,' Nikolai was saying. 'You're only sixteen.'

'They don't know that,' Evheny says in reply. 'I look older.'

Vitaly stands behind them. Secretly he is worried. He cannot sign any forms. He does not know how.

The SS in the shade of the recruiting tent do not even ask Evheny's age. They slide some forms towards him, and are surprised when he starts to read them. The two Germans look at each other, then at the dark-eyed boy reading the forms. They are fair young men, the well-educated elite of the *Einsatzgruppen*. They watch as the scruffy Ukrainian locals are fed in one end of the recruiting tent to emerge at the other end washed and scrubbed, with bowl haircuts and German uniforms.

'You're holding up the works, boy. There's others waiting.'

'Sorry, er, Sir.' He fills out the form hurriedly, signs it, and joins the queue being led into the tent. He sees Nikolai up ahead, his beard shaven and his curls ruthlessly sheared off, leaving just a patch on the top of his head.

Vitaly leans over the desk. He notices the two Germans admiring his hair and eyes. They shove the form towards him. The day is beginning to get both hot and boring: the loud-speaker announcements, coupled with marching music, dragged in more work than they had anticipated. Vitaly stares at the paper blankly. The two Germans start to titter. The form is upside down.

'You can't fill in the form?'

Vitaly shakes his head, burning with shame.

'I wouldn't worry. You're not alone.' The more senior of the two Germans takes it, gripping his fountain pen with the assurance of regular use. 'Get a move on up there, you lot,' Vitaly hears from some distance in the queue behind him.

'Name?'

'Vitaly Fyodorovich Kovalenko.'

'Age?'

'Nineteen.'

'Date of birth.'

'October 17th, 1921.'

'Any family?'

'No, sir.'

The German looks up. 'You related to the last fellow?'

'Yes. He's my brother.'

'Put your mark here,' he indicates. Vitaly's calloused index finger smudges the ink.

'Good. Proceed.'

Proceed. The process is started, and the village looks on with pride at its young men in their smart German uniforms. Vitaly sees his mother alternately clasping her cheeks and her chest. 'That's my two boys!' The Germans are taking down information from the mothers. One of the Germans says 'There are no men in this village. It's strange. No men. Only women and children.' The men children sit along temporary benches, duffle bags on their laps, combing what is left of their hair. They chatter, wondering what they will have to do, where they will have to go. The women children look at them admiringly. Finally, trucks come and take them to Khmel'nik, where the process is continued.

IN THE town of Khmel'nik, the recruits from the village were split into two groups. The Germans sent the first group to Poland, to work in the vicinity of Lublin. 'Important work' was to be carried out in Poland, which the Nazis felt should be done by 'savage people', not by the good Germans themselves. The second group was sent to Kiev, where the work was even more 'important', because it was 'urgent'. Vitaly found that he and Evheny had been separated. Vitaly would go to Poland. Evheny would go to Kiev. Evheny found out the name of the Ukrainian Militia training camp near Lublin from one of the German officers: Trawniki SS Training Camp. And then he stood patiently while another German photographed all the men from Kolkhoz number 28 in a compact group shot. Evheny stood beside his tall brother as the young and gangly German with the camera took their photo. The German grinned, showing a set of rotting, crooked teeth. 'I'll get the snaps developed in Kiev. My name's Rottenführer Wagner, yes, first name Tristan. Viking. Anyone who wants a print put their name and serial number down here on this clipboard. I'll get them to you in Kiev.'

Vitaly looked at his brother. 'You'll get a photo, won't you? We don't have a photo of ourselves at all.' Evheny said. 'I'll go one better. In Kiev, I'll buy a camera like that German's got.'

VITALY: They told us we would be free, and that no one would kill us anymore. That we would not starve. That we would have our country. We believed them. I and my brother joined them, early on. They gave us nothing like they promised: good food yes, clothes and things yes, but no country. No hope. They got us to do the shitwork that they didn't want to do themselves. And then it was too late. If you disagreed with a German he shot you. So you did what you were told. In the morning they gave you so much drink you didn't know what you were doing. During the day you drank more so you forgot. Then after a while you didn't feel anything inside, nothing at all. You thought you were normal again but you weren't. You can't feel. You think you can but you can't.

KATERYNA: When we reached the city of Kiev, the Germans housed many of the refugees in the offices and apartments that once belonged to Communist Party functionaries. They themselves took the best accommodation. I had never seen the beautiful city of Kiev before, and was surprised to note that the Bolshies had not torn down all the churches—only most of them. Admittedly, those that remained had been closed, but the Nazis soon opened them again, allowing their dusty bells to peal out across the landscape. There is a legend which states that all the church bells of Kiev rung together can be heard twenty miles away. I don't know if this is true, but the celebratory ringing was certainly very loud.

Hasse appropriated a pleasant apartment overlooking Konstantinovskaya Street, where the cinema was located. The bed was made up with real cotton sheets, and the pillows—of which there where about half-a-dozen—were fringed with white lace. The bedroom had a clean white telephone in it, with a printed message beside it stating that all phone calls to Germany, Denmark and Holland were 'on the Reich' until the 30th of September. Presumably this was so that the soldiers and their officers could contact their families and sweethearts at home in the West. I had no one I could contact, so I sat and looked dumbly at the receiver. Beside the phone was a little lamp with a frosted-glass lampshade. A switch on the side allowed you to brighten or dim the intensity of the light. I fiddled and played with this technological miracle while Hasse was showering and singing the 'Horst Wessel Song' at top volume. The apartment had water pumped right into the kitchen, and the floor was carpeted with a thick pile the colour of vanilla ice-cream. I rubbed my bare feet back and forth on it, amazed at its softness. Hasse stepped out of the bathroom, a towel tucked around his middle, rubbing his head with another, smaller towel. 'Right. It's your turn. Watch the hot water tap, you don't have to turn it too far before you scald yourself.'

'Hot water?'

He looked at me. 'Haven't you had a hot shower before, girl?'

'No, sir.'

'Don't give me that "sir" bullshit. Come here.'

I followed him meekly. He opened the door to a perfectly clean, tiled bathroom. One of the tiles had a hammer and sickle decal on it. Willie chuckled. 'Sorry about the decorations, but we're working on it.' The floor was tiled in tasteful pale green. The bathroom fittings were designed along a 'sea' theme. A shell-shaped holder held a cake of soap. The taps above the sink were carefully designed to resemble fish. The walls of the bathroom were white and pristine. He pointed at the shower. 'Observe. Hot tap.' He spoke with humorous officiousness. The fittings in the shower were brass, but otherwise normal—not shaped like fish. They too gleamed. 'Now. Cold tap. See up there. Shower rose. Turn on cold tap first. Always turn on cold tap first, unless one wants to boil oneself.' He turned on the cold tap. 'Now, turn on hot tap,' he did so. 'Wait until water is right temperature. Then get in the shower. Well. Go on.' He clearly expected me to undress before him, and I did so, slowly. He waited, taking my Komsomol uniform from me. 'This,' he said, with care and precision, 'is going in the incinerator.'

'But I don't have any other clothes.'

'Never mind. Get in the shower. And wash your hair. There's shampoo up there.' He indicated a niche in the tiled wall. He left, closing the door behind him. I scrubbed myself under the warm water, and scrubbed my hair. Dirt and rubbish flowed down the plughole. When I emerged, I took two of the white towels as he had done and dried my body and my hair separately. My hair had only ever been washed a few times before, and never with real shampoo. It now fanned out ridiculously. Strawberry blond curls hung damply over my shoulders. Pieces of short hair stuck out at odd angles.

It was then that I saw the dress.

ERICH Kretschmann watched as, two days later, Hasse came down the wide steps, schoolgirl-turned woman on his arm. She was wearing a peach-coloured evening gown, and Hasse was in his dress uniform. He smoked a cigar that was, by its quality, distinctly black market. They looked fresh and lively, not at all like people who had been screwing for the last forty-eight hours solid. Her light red hair was piled up in a massive French roll on one side of her head. Her face was prettily though inexpertly made up. Hasse took her into the officers' dining room, to show her off. *Look what I found in my breakfast cereal.* Kretschmann thrust his hands deep into his pockets and followed his commander into the mess, his head down. He had dreamt again last night. A great, lurid, scaly basilisk from medieval mythology had spoken to him. 'I really don't want to vaporise you with my breath, but I am a basilisk, and I cannot escape from my nature,' it had said, quite kindly, not looking directly at him. 'Basilisks, if they breathe on anything, even something they like, it turns into a little pile of cinders. I cannot even look at you, and yet I like you. I don't want to turn you into soot. I want to be a certain thing: kind and good, but I cannot. You also want to be a certain thing. Isn't it strange?' Then the monster had looked at him, and he awoke just as his hair was catching on fire, one hand clutching his head, sweating monstrously. He looked out onto the street. The synagogue across the road was burning fiercely. He was afraid now. He remembered the painting that his mother had suspended above his bed when he was a small child. It showed a giant, unblinking human eye within a triangular border, and bore on the blank space beneath the eye an inscription: 'Thou God Seest Me'. Thou God seest me. He pulled the sodden sheets up under his chin, and prayed.

KATERYNA: Often Jews and Bolsheviks were placed in German army lorries below our third-storey window, thence to be displayed throughout the city, where some people threw mud at them and laughed while others just stared fixedly. Many of the people so displayed had once occupied positions of authority in the city of Kiev, and the townsfolk were still afraid of them. Some of the senior Germans said to Willie that Ukrainians had no spirit; if they hated these people so much, why did they do nothing about them now? But the staring was from shock and amazement. Sky and soil had just changed places, which, you will agree, is a very serious thing.

I saw the young cadre leader from Leningrad displayed one day, saw her taken around to the secluded rear of the Udarnik cinema by two Ukrainian militia men, or '*Hilfswillige*' as the Germans liked to call them. 'Willing to help', it meant. There, behind the cinema, the two men raped her, taking turns. I know that the Germans officially forbade this, because it violated their Race and Resettlement Act, but when there was no German supervision, the '*Hiwis*' would do as they pleased. Finally, they shot her in the head, and loaded her corpse onto the back of the lorry. A handsome, heavily built Cossack with a machine pistol in his hands guarded the other people in the lorry. He sat smoking a cigarette on the tailboard of the truck, his arms draped loosely over his knees. I looked closely at one of the rapists as he stood to button his fly; his crinkly, light-brown hair seemed familiar. He looked up, unintentionally, towards my window.

'Evheny! Evheny! Up here! Look up here! on the third floor!' I pushed the window out to its fullest extent, my hands shaking, and leaned out. He would behave if he saw me. 'It's me, Kateryna!'

He waved from where he stood on the pavement, shouting in return. Then, without warning, both he and his comrade turned and sprinted up the street and out of sight. The Cossack looked towards the sound of their booted steps and shouted, leaning around the side of the truck. 'Hey you fuckers! Come back here! Come back!' He shrugged his shoulders indifferently when they ignored him, and said something to the lorry driver. The lorry began to grind slowly up the street. The corpse of the cadre leader threatened to slide off the tailboard and the Cossack grabbed it by the hair, hauling it backwards on the swaying vehicle. The dozen or so Jews in the lorry moved timidly out of his way as he pushed the body up against the rear of the cab. He resumed his seat on the tailgate, removed his fur cap and began to comb his matted shoulder-length hair and fiddle with his long moustache. *The Germans have not made the old Tsarists cut their hair.* I looked at the corpse. Its eyes were open, and blood ran out of its mouth. I felt a twinge in my ribs, and looked away. My throat was dry, I shut my eyes and could see only that pale death mask. I stood up, and put my shoulders back. *Ukrainians do not act like cattle.*

The next day, the streets of Kiev were full of Jews dragging their belongings behind them, marching slowly towards the Kiev football stadium. But they were to be taken eventually to Babii-Yar, a big sandy ravine near the river Dnieper, divested of first their belongings, then their clothes, and finally their lives. The Germans and militia shot the Jews from across the yar with machine-guns set up on tripods. Even though many people nearby could hear what was going on, or could see from top-floor apartment windows, they said nothing. You didn't know if this was just something between the Jews and the Germans. This was how the massacre could continue the next day. More Jews obeyed the order to assemble for resettlement, and queued up peacefully to die. Only when they were twenty metres or so away from their deaths did the Germans allow the Ukrainian militia—some still partly clad in Soviet uniforms, a fact which annoyed Willie—to beat them senseless with lumps of timber. Allow Rottweilers and Dobermans to tear them partly to pieces. 'If there is one thing I cannot stand, it is politically incorrect dress,' Willie told me.

EVHENY is standing in the corridor of militia leading to the yar. Alex Voronikov is beside him, chewing a stick of wheat. Voronikov has a big, slow smile, and the sprig of wheat moves up and down with his jaw as he chews. He likes Evheny, 'smart-arse', as he calls him. He and half-a-dozen others had Evheny up until the wee hours the night before reading bits of poetry, old newspapers, and German anti-Semitic ordinances. 'Jews will not pollute the Ostvolk, for they are the Führer's friends.' Voronikov has been to school, for a whole two years, longer than Evheny, but he can barely read the alphabet. This is because he was malnourished at the time, and was too preoccupied with the gaping hole in his stomach to learn his letters. He does not really know this. He is just stupid—that is what the teachers said. Just plain stupid. He tucks his hair behind his ears. The pretty German girl who is in charge of sorting the Jewish clothing into neat and ordered piles is looking at him. He smiles at her, his best woman-melting smile, showing his lovely straight teeth, his 'best point'. She smiles back. He makes a mental note to see her during the break. The Germans said there would be a break. They have even supplied some vodka—half-a-litre per Ukrainian. Voronikov has already consumed this, but he knows where he can get more.

Evheny sees his sister arrive in a chauffeur-driven BMW coupé, beside a handsome German officer. She kisses the officer on the mouth before he leaves the car. He kisses her gently on the palm as the door is opened for him. Voronikov elbows Evheny in the ribs. Hard. The German is walking towards them, giving instructions in a low, pleasant voice. The car drives away down the street, slowly. Soldiers move to let it pass.

KATERYNA: Willie did not want to upset me with evil sights, so he ordered the car back to our apartment. He did not want me to see anything, despite the fact that everyone knew what was going on. Even the Jews and communists knew, but now it was too late for them. This annoyed me, at the time, but in retrospect I am glad I did not see what happened at Babii-Yar. The hands of people who had always been oppressed grew wild. Communists had told them 'grow this' and they had done so. Communists had said 'give us your crops' and they had meekly complied. When the men were beaten stupid in the streets, the women would patch them up and watch them drink their spirit sadly away. Then they would be beaten themselves. By drunken husbands. By communists. Even their children were a type of punishment, because they kept dying. So now the hands that had gently nurtured seedlings into growth gripped and tore. The same gentle people who cooed lullabies to their surviving babies took more than verbal revenge on those more fortunate in times past. I could barely hear the machine-guns because of the methods the Germans used in locating and firing them, but I well knew what was happening, as did everyone. People walked around with knowing faces, and spoke in knowing voices. German soldiers would politely ask the way to 'the Babii-Yar', and people would politely give them directions. No one was rude.

Below my window, I heard such a conversation. Two SS men with pale, uncaring eyes and white, intoxicated faces were pestering old Irka the cloth-seller for instructions. Irka gabbled quickly in Ukrainian, indicating the right direction with her knobbly fingers. Suddenly, one of the men vomited on the pavement in front of her stall. Pale green, like his eyes, the puke was. His companion guided him away. Irka did not laugh. She did not smile. But she did not shake her head.

KRETSCHMANN crouches behind his machine-gun again. His hands are blistered. His shoulders are stiff with painful cramps. He feels ill. His mind is full of visions. The autumn day is warm and sticky. The shooting has given him a headache, and his mouth is clogged with phlegm. He sees out of the corner of his eye the Ukrainian Police with blue and yellow 'Organisation of Ukrainian Nationalists' armbands. They form a corridor and beat the Jews in manageable groups towards the yar with sawn-off pool cues and iron bars. They are covered with blood. Their uniforms are an interesting mix of blood, Soviet stars and Nazi eagles.

He notices one in particular, a big, lean, curly-headed youth with brown skin and high cheekbones who holds his iron bar in one hand so that he may still his victim with the other. Kretschmann stands, the blood rushes from his head. 'Hey you! Big boy!' The youth stands up straight, swaying unsteadily. Kretschmann thinks he's drunk. Drunk and crazy. Kretschmann halts the arrival of the next group of Jews with his hand. They are held back, shivering and crying, by the bloody Ukrainians. 'You. You come and use the machine-gun.' The boy does not understand, and Kretschmann momentarily curses his inability to speak Ukrainian. He beckons. 'You. Curly-top. Come here.' He points to the weapon. The others in the corridor of Ukrainians eye the boy with envy, and push him forward. 'Go on, Voronikov. He wants you.' Voronikov walks around the yar, towards the yellow-eyed German with curly brown hair like his own, an alcoholic smile on his lips, his bar across his shoulders, his hands hooked over it. He staggers once or twice, and as he looks up the beckoning German acquires two heads and a silver halo. He stops before Kretschmann. Kretschmann stands, dwarfed by the youth. He reaches up and touches the boy's eyes, and then the weapon. 'Watch. I will show you only once.' Jews are beaten through the corridor. Kretschmann and his comrades fire. The Jews collapse into the ravine. He shows the boy how to reload. He stands, brushing his pants, pointing to the machine-gun. The boy looks at him as if to say *now?* Kretschmann nods. *Yes, now.* He sees the boozy glint in the boy's green eyes, the uncomprehending grin on his face. The boy's comrades manning the corridor yell and whistle, wielding their poles with alcoholic ferocity. One of them is sick. Voronikov bends and fires. Kretschmann watches as, strong as he his, Voronikov is unprepared for the violent movement of the machine-gun. His head jerks back, briefly, but he is determined to gain control. Kretschmann turns his back on the yar, and walks towards the vehicles and mobile infirmary of *Einsatzgruppe* C. The Ukrainians are whistling now, a high pitched and oddly melodic sound. Kretschmann holds his face in his hands.

In the ranks of the *Einsatzgruppen*, one does not take a 'sickie'. One takes a 'mental health day'. This is a joke, but it is meant in all seriousness. Hasse sneers at Kretschmann from behind a cloud of cigarette smoke. 'Having a mental health day, Erich?' Kretschmann salutes weakly, pushing past him, vomiting on the black earth. He looks up as he pulls off his cap. Nine other SS men are in there with him. The ground is covered with vomit. One cries, hysterically, words tumbling out in Czech and German. 'They can do it oh let them do it they don't care.' Another stares at the wall. Tears. Vomit. Another man follows Kretschmann into the infirmary. 'I got one of those bloody peasants to take over I'm sorry but I can't handle this.' Kretschmann is sick again. There is conversation above. He hears Hasse laugh. 'Don't some people give you the shits? Yes, it's such a shame. Such a shame.'

A NEUROPSYCHIATRIST who has had the opportunity to analyse members of the *Einsatzgruppen* reports 'twenty per cent of the Einsatzgruppen suffered significant psychological difficulties due to their participation.' Kretschmann does not know this now, but he will, after the war. He remembers how as a second-year medical student he enlisted in the SS. He was angry, then. Until Babii-Yar, he had believed quite faithfully in it, but now, he crashes to the ground in a dead faint.

Later he will go back to Germany and raise his Polish-born

son in Munich. He will hate racism, and will not worry when his son becomes politically involved with anarchists. It is when he goes to a Beatles concert in 1964—he is young, only mid-forties, and their music is to his liking as well as his son's—that he is reminded, terribly. The manic fervour. The ecstatic faces, particularly of the young. Before this, he will go mad, and ask to be transferred to the most dangerous front, east or west. He will try to die, but will fail. After the war he will finish his degree in medicine. He will join the Peace Corps. He will minister to the poorest, the most disadvantaged. He will finally be killed in Angola, by South African-backed UNITA rebels. He will always hear the melodic drunken whistling of the Ukrainians combined with the sad strains of 'The nowhere man'. When he dies, the last image he will see is that of the big curly-headed corn-fed boy with the strong, white teeth, with just a hint of murder in his sloe green eyes.

KATERYNA: It was only later I heard that there were many Ukrainians who tried to save Jews from their fate at Babii-Yar. Some were well aware that the Germans did not intend to grant Ukraine any sort of independence: the whole country was slated for German colonisation. They said that German propaganda and Soviet propaganda were identical horseshit. Barsek Ohlobla, who came from my own village, was one of these Ukrainians. Underneath my window, when Willie was at the yar, I saw Barsek guiding Jews away from the city centre, plucking them out of the slow-marching columns. At first I thought he was saving Jews he knew, but then I realised that he was taking those Jews who did not look Jewish—people who could hide most easily using Aryan papers. When night came I went downstairs and watched Barsek and his compatriots hard at work. The Cossack sentry appointed to guard that portion of the crowd lay stretched out on the footpath, snoring. His face was very smooth and gentle in the moonlight. There was an empty vodka bottle in the gutter beside him. Barsek looked up at me.

'Kateryna Fyodorovna. I suppose you'll report me.'

'For helping communists, yes.'

One of the old Jews seated in the roadway looked at Barsek. 'So it is true. They mean to kill us.' Barsek wrung his hands. I noticed that his blond hair was shot through with grey, and that his eyes were clouded. He spoke to the old Jew very softly.

'They have been killing you all day. And many of my people are secretly very happy about it. They cannot forgive Kaganovich for what he has done. I am sorry. I am truly sorry.'

'But I did not cause the famine!'

I felt bile collecting in my mouth. The hate came flooding out now and I couldn't stop it. I said, 'No, but you did not starve the way we did. My father and brother, and three of my uncles and two of my aunts and their children died in it. Your family is doubtless complete.'

The Jew wailed. Barsek slapped him on the back of the head with his open palm. 'Quiet! You'll wake our Cossack friend here, and he will kill. I want to save you, not see you shot!'

'Why do you save them? They are worthless communists.'

Barsek pointed at a small child curled sleeping in the arms of its terrified mother near his feet.

'Kateryna, is that a communist?'

I felt shame then, and made to walk upstairs, but Barsek stepped over the body of the sleeping Cossack and stopped in front of me.

'Don't you go anywhere. I want to tell you something.' He bunched my blouse in his fist. 'That German who you seem to enjoy fucking so much is supervising a great slaughter. Not just communists but anyone else who doesn't fit in with Hitler's twisted idea of perfection. At first I thought all right, communist Jews, we don't need them, get rid of them. But children? Babies? Wilhelm Hasse must be on very intimate terms with the Devil, because he seems to enjoy it, do you know that? And your brother Evheny is helping the Germans with their despicable business at the yar, and your other brother Vitaly has joined the Waffen SS also. I saw him in the SS recruiting tent. In Khmel'nik.'

His voice rose continually as he spoke. He tapped at my chest with his index finger, emphasising his points. Only a loud grunting noise from the Cossack guardsman as he was disturbed in his sleep halted the flow of Barsek's eloquence. He spat on the concrete at my feet and strode away.

In the end, someone must have reported them. Even though Hitler had made Ukrainians 'honorary Aryans', they were still taken to Babii-Yar and machine-gunned into the pit. Later the Gestapo came for their families and their children. Willie stayed away from the Gestapo officers and smoked his cigars. He said he did not like them.

I also learned that Barsek alone somehow managed to escape from the pit at Babii-Yar; he had been shot in the arm and hand, but the people doing the shooting were so drunk that they did not notice and did not try to finish him off or properly cover him with earth. He climbed out of the ravine and sneaked his way into the hills in the north. He became a partisan, in the Ukrainska Povstancha Armia, the UPA. Everywhere he went he showed potential recruits the hole in his left palm, stigmata of the German shame.

SHURA was captured south of Kiev, during the rapid Nazi advance south of the city. The Germans marched him and some fifteen thousand others to a former Soviet Army training camp, and ordered them to sit in the dirt and wait. SS men came and asked the ordinary soldiers to point out the Jews and political kommissars. These men were separated from the main group and shot. Many of the prisoners cheered. The SS then divided the rest of the prisoners into two groups, Russian and non-Russian. The Russians were marched away and loaded onto trains near the camp. The Ukrainians, Kazakhs and Latvians were left under a loose guard.

Later a grey-haired SS man dressed in a smart, black uniform drove up in an armoured car and asked, quite blatantly, for 400 anti-Semitic Ukrainians and Latvians. The Wehrmacht could have the rest, he said. He only wanted 400. The Wehrmacht guards asked no questions, and simply numbered off 400 Ukrainians and Latvians. Shura was pushed into this group. They were so careless that they accidentally included about thirty Kazakhs in the selection, but the SS officer did not seem to worry. Then he ordered them to stand, and they were marched around the perimeter of the camp, and ordered to sit in a group. The SS man stood in front of them. 'I will be back shortly, and you will be taken to a training camp. You are needed for a very important task. You will be trained for this purpose.' Another SS man, with a round Ukrainian face, stood before him and translated his words into Russian, so that even the Kazakhs would have some idea of what was going on. 'There will be plenty of food, vodka and sex,' he continued. The Ukrainian translator was grinning as he relayed the words. 'And you will be part of a great and historic mission.' The Latvians and Kazakhs were beginning to like the idea, and applauded. They liked the well-dressed German warriors with their neat uniforms and shining insignia, their idealism, their bravado. The Ukrainians stared with their mouths open. The translator began to laugh out loud. 'You'll all catch flies if you keep that up.' Shura looked at the translator's head. Gentle rain was falling and it beaded his long, feminine eyelashes. His moon face was shining and wet.

Shura sat in the dirt, chasing flies out of his eyes. Half-a-dozen bored-looking Wehrmacht soldiers stood guard around the group of which he was a part. The transport was taking its time. He stared out over the flat countryside, scratching his filthy head. His empty stomach rumbled. The crops were black, the soil smelled of kerosene. A farmhouse a few hundred metres distant was a gutted shell.

One of the soldiers guarding in a rather desultory manner leaned on his rifle and stared at them, shaking his head sadly. He looked at his watch, and strolled away from the group, glancing down the road. A dozen lorries, marked on the side with the double lightning standard of the SS, made their way towards the Ukrainians and Latvians seated in the dust. The Wehrmacht soldier who had stood apart from them now turned. 'Here's your lift,' he yelled, grimacing, adding the words 'You poor stupid sods.' The lorries halted and a dozen SS men directed the group towards them. They piled gratefully inside, seating themselves on the wooden benches. Shura stood stiffly, wiping his muddy hands on the pants of his Soviet uniform. One of the SS men stood beside him. 'You too, yellow fellow,' he said kindly, in bad Russian. 'You'll feel better when we arrive.'

The Wehrmacht soldiers joined the SS in the cabs of the trucks. Shura found himself beside a boy of about seventeen who now began to cry. He put his arm around the boy's thin shoulders, trying to console him. The child looked up, licking parched lips. 'I don't care about any Jews,' he whined. 'I'm hungry, and I'm thirsty, and I want to go home.' Four hours later, on dusk, they reached a group of neat buildings encircled by barbed wire.

In front was a sign which welcomed them to Trawniki SS training camp in fancy black Gothic print, in both German and Russian. They were taken inside and directed towards the showers, where the Germans kindly asked them not to run the hot-water system dry. Later they were sent to the mess hall, already crowded with Ukrainians who had arrived some weeks earlier, and who were washed and scrubbed and wearing German-supplied uniforms. They themselves were supplied with an odd assortment of clean civilian clothes. Shura even saw one man in a skirt. They queued obediently for their dinner, a substantial feed of pork and potatoes, and sat at the trestle tables, eating greedily. The boy seemed happier now he was washed and full. He started to sing, his light tenor voice going out high and clear into the soft October night. Others joined in. The Germans passed bottles of vodka among them, and the singing got louder. The Latvians sang a Lutheran hymn. 'A mighty fortress is our God', it ran. 'A trusty shield and weapon.' The tall German who had spoken to them at the POW camp appeared and finally settled them down, and after apologising for the delay, told them of their new roles. The translator stood and rendered his words into Russian.

'Welcome to the Waffen SS. I am Sturmbannführer Streibel, your commanding officer. Here, as I mentioned earlier, you will be taught important tasks. Our Führer, Adolf Hitler, admires the anti-Semitism of Ukrainians and Latvians greatly, and wants anti-Semites across Europe to unite. However, your anti-Semitism must be put to productive uses. We cannot build the New Europe without your help. You will be paid well and clothed warmly. When you are posted, you will have to work hard, but the rewards are worthwhile.' He grinned salaciously. There was a moment of confusion as the translator explained the meaning of 'anti-Semitism'. Then the Latvians cheered, thumping the table and stomping their feet. 'There will be plenty to eat and drink.' Cheers from the Ukrainians. 'And you will have one week's leave for every three months' work, as well as some off-duty times.' Riotous applause. One of the Kazakhs rocked back so far that he fell off his chair.

The boy looked into Shura's face, smiling. 'Will they let me see my mum?' he asked. Shura nodded. 'Of course they will. You'll be able to buy presents for your mum.' The German continued. 'After your important task is complete, you will be returned to your villages and farms. You will enjoy the fruits of your labour.' The applause was now amplified with hoots and whistles. Some felt apprehensive, but the room was so warm and the food so plentiful that the Germans just *had* to be the best people in the world. The majority slopped hungrily away at the meal before them, even the Muslim Kazakhs, and Streibel smiled. 'After you've eaten, we will show you your living quarters. Lights out is at 2100 hours. The Führer wants you to be up in the morning for exercises. He wants to build young, healthy bodies. You will be fitted with uniforms tomorrow, also. Like these others,' he indicated the already uniformed group who sat off to one side. 'These brothers have been with us for three whole weeks. And I assure all of you that not all nights will be this early.' He smiled again, knowingly, drawing more cheers from the Latvians. He raised his right arm, stiffly, with steady majesty. '*Sieg Heil! Heil Hitler!*' The diners rose quickly, imitating him, making the roof ring with the new chant, even though their pronunciation lacked a little formality. He left them to eat the rest of their dinner in noisy camaraderie, turning to his German orderly as he exited. 'Good God,' he said. 'What savages!'

Shura wiped his mouth on the back of his hand and followed the uniformed blond Ukrainian who had been appointed to direct his table of forty or so to the barracks. 'Come on,' the young man said, flicking a piece of perfect golden hair out of his eyes. 'It's good here. Lots of food. Although it's been all early nights so far.'

Shura drew level with him, struggling to keep pace with his long strides. He waited. Everyone was besieging the young man with questions.

'What do we have to do?'

'How much do we get paid?'

'Where do we get sent?'

Shura found out that the young man was Vitaly, and that his best friend was Nikolai, who wanted to buy a car, and that there were a dozen others from villages around

Khmel'nik. He said he once knew a girl from Khmel'nik, a Kateryna, and soon there was an exciting discovery. Brothers and Sisters! Clichés about the smallness of the world were exchanged, copious quantities of vodka were consumed, and in the morning Kommandant Streibel marvelled at the discovery of an entire race that did not suffer from hangovers. Vitaly and Nikolai called Shura 'yella fella', which he hated but couldn't avoid. He was not as yellow as the Kazakhs in the next barrack, but he could have been taken for one at a pinch.

ALSO IN the morning, the lessons begin.

This is the uniform. It is very smart, black, a handsome hat with a silver skull emblem on it, fine shiny buttons, a sleeve patch with a salamander on the yellow and blue of the Ukrainian flag. March in the solemn and stirring parade. Admire yourself in the mirror, boys. Respect yourselves.

This is the village. There are Jews in there. This is a tactical exercise. You will go in pairs into the houses and tell the Jews to get dressed, tell them to take whatever they can. Then you will put them on the train, as many as you can. The trains will take them to Lublin and Treblinka.

This is a rifle. No, you thickheaded Ukrainian savage, you don't look down the skinny end and wonder why it doesn't work, unless you want a face like crushed watermelon. That's better. You spring the catch like this. Good. We will play music while you shoot them. It sounds like very loud static in a radio broadcast. You don't want to shoot them? Too bad. You obey. And yes, you must only shoot them when we tell you. There must be no waste. Each bullet costs the Reich three pfennigs. You don't know Mozart? Such a shame. Yes, you can sing.

This is a death camp. Your post is in Sobibor, yours in Treblinka, yours in Belzec, yours in Majdanek. Yes, the leave arrangements are still the same. No, you won't have to come back here unless you stuff up. Yes, some of you will be sent to the Warsaw Ghetto to supervise things there, but that is only temporary.

This is your late night, as promised. It is your farewell to Trawniki. The women have been paid for by the Reich. They are from the fine Polish city of Lublin. You are to have a good time with them, but no one is to be hurt, or I will deal with the perpetrators in a manner which I feel is appropriate. Now go to it.

'In the villages, they call us "Askaris". What does that mean?'
    'African, I believe. From East Africa, it means a fighter and tribesman for the Empire. Anything wild, uncivilised. That is what it means.'

SHURA, yella fella, is sent immediately to Treblinka. Vitaly and Nikolai work for one month in the Warsaw Ghetto, in the sticky summer, then are transferred to Treblinka, where there is a lot of killing going on. Alex Voronikov, a carpenter, is set the task of supervising some Jewish labourers. He is widely reported to be a bastard, but no one cares.

DURING the deportations from the ghetto, Jews with industrial work passes are not to be removed from the ghetto precinct. However, some of these work-Jews try to smuggle their children past the Germans and Ukrainians at the checkpoints around the ghetto, rather than see them sent away. They chloroform their babies and hide them in knapsacks, and one bright, hot day, a knapsack on a father's back mysteriously starts to cry. The people filing past freeze. The German in charge of the selection lets fly with a stream of filth that makes even Nikolai blush to the roots of his black hair. 'You cocksucker! What the fuck do you think you're going to do? Keep

your cunts of kids away from here!' The Jew is the colour of
pale puke, his eyes roll up in his head. Vitaly looks at the
pallid face, and in the passage of a second, feels immensely
sorry for this man with a round, sensitive mouth and thin
hair and pathetic, frightened eyes. *How can something be so
nasty and so nice at the same time?* He experiences a series of
feelings in that second. Pity. Fear. Longing. Power. Hate. He
lunges forward, his long fingers fixing his bayonet. He drives
it into the knapsack. Blood runs down his arms, splashes his
face and hair. He hears nothing of the wild screams around
him, sees nothing of the other Ukrainians trying to keep some
sort of order. He stops. The Jew crashes to the pavement, his
eyes wide. His body curled foetally. The German is hitting
him with his whip, over and over again. Vitaly levels his rifle,
and in what he will always consider to be an act of mercy,
shoots the man between the eyes.

THE BROTHERS Kovalenko and their comrades—Nikolai and
Shura—did not kill Jews just because they were poor and
Ukrainian, and did not know any better. They killed Jews
because they believed that they themselves were savages.

This learned savagery was compounded by the Nazis, who
rewarded it where no rewards had been forthcoming in the
past. Vitaly received a bonus for finding the baby in the
knapsack with his bayonet, which he went and spent in the
city on vodka and a prostitute. Nikolai stopped beating his
wife, and would bring her gifts and fancy foods. They had
fought, in the past, in a silent, grimacing fashion. The domestic violence that wakes the neighbours and makes them look
through the windows at the quarrelling shadows was not in
their line. They thumped at each other's flesh with kitchen
implements and occasionally, iron pokers. But now there was
plenty of money and food, the fights stopped. Poles would
watch as the short, muscular Ukrainian would walk to his

lodgings each Friday evening, take about fifteen minutes to wash and change, then emerge to promenade in summer with his pretty wife on his arm, she holding the hand of a playful five-year-old. So regular was this that people would comment 'Time to put the fish on, there goes the *Hiwi* and his wife.' Evheny was given lessons in German, so that his commander could leave the rest of the militiamen under his authority. He stole Meissen, Swarovski and Bohemia from the Jewish houses he looted, sending it priority post to his mother in Khmel'nik. Shura found himself taken frequently to Soviet prisoner-of-war camps, where he would induce others like himself to take the Nazi side. He tried to warn them on more than one occasion that they would be beaten and starved to death if they did not, but he was not usually successful.

The Germans in Treblinka admired their singing savages, to the point that clever Dr Imfried Eberl, the first Kommandant, developed a theory. 'You know,' he would say, 'I have a funny feeling that oppressed people free themselves through their music. Look at the Negroes in America. My Ukrainians are the same. Listen to them, like birds!' He was so convinced of this that he organised a choir among the Ukrainians who patrolled the Warsaw Ghetto. His choir was a success. Even the Jews who daily suffered indignities at the hands of the Ukrainians in the district acknowledged the quality of their choir. The Jews called them 'Nightingales'. So, the three groups of savages that made daily, murderous incursions into the ghetto would be hailed as 'Litts, Latts and Nightingales'. Several times, the Ukrainians performed for the inhabitants of Aryan Warsaw, in the neat clipped public parks, and here the Poles found themselves assailed with stunning renditions of 'Shenandoah' and 'Swing low, Sweet chariot' in the midst of a German and Ukrainian repertoire. The *Kapellmeister* would always kindly explain that this singing of enemy songs was simply to display the vocal talent of 'his' Nightingales.

Two to three times a week, the Ukrainians would saunter

off to choir practice, singing as they went, performing impromptu recitals in the street for anyone who cared to listen. The Poles, Christians all, usually listened. *They are rapists and murderers, but it was the Heavenly Father who gave them their voices. Praise Him.*

VITALY stops before the liquor shop, his bonus in hand. He looks in the window and slowly ascends the wooden steps to Popławski's Liquor Supplies. The tall Pole who runs the shop unbends from behind the counter, standing upright, wispy grey hair clinging to his oily head. A brown-eyed portrait of the Virgin Mary decorates the green, peeling paint of the far wall. He sees an even taller Askari, blood on his uniform and in his hair, rubbing a significant amount of occupation złoty together in his hands. 'Yes?' he asks. 'May I help you?'

Vitaly points, silently, to the 'Premium Quality Russian Vodka' displayed behind the Pole and holds up two fingers, proud of his ability to fool the Pole into thinking he can read the small handwritten sign. Popławski sees that he does not need to talk to this man. His people seldom have anything to say. He fulfils the order, wrapping the bottles up in a brown paper bag. The Askari holds the złoty over the counter in the manner of one unaccustomed to handling money, forcing Popławski to scrape it from his damp palm. Popławski watches as he leaves the store, skilfully unscrewing the cap on the first bottle with one hand, then tilting his head back and drinking. About two hundred metres down the road is a fairly classy brothel, located above a clothing store. A small sign, made of light bulbs, flashes 'OPEN OPEN OPEN'. Popławski watches as the Askari strides inside.

Vitaly steps in, blinded by the dark and smoke. He has bought two lovely orgasms with Popławski's 'Premium Quality Russian Vodka'. Now he may purchase a third.

THREE

'Why did you kill the whole family?'
'They was home!'

murderer on death row, in response to a
question tabled by Richard Pryor.

To choose one's victims, to prepare one's plan
minutely, to slake an implacable vengeance,
and then to go to bed. . . There is nothing
sweeter in the world.

Stalin

The lawyer. The lawyer. My sister is getting the lawyer. I meet
my sister Natalya in the Queen Street Mall, as planned. She
is sitting on the steps of the band rotunda, reading a novel. I
stop in front of her. We hug, exchange a few pleasantries. She
is a handsome woman, my sister. Her pretty, foxy face is
brightly made-up, her eye shadow carefully matching her
dark maroon slacks suit. She wears one gold fingernail to be
'eccentric'.

She asks, 'Where's Vitaly?'

'Gone shopping with Mum,' I say. 'In David Jones. He

doesn't own a suit. He's determined to go to court in a suit.'
I ask, 'Have you got the lawyer?'

'Yes. Listen. Down here.'

We walk down a flight of steps shooting out from the side of the Mall into a Thai restaurant, and order some dinner. Next door is a McDonald's, then a Kentucky Fried. In the moist streets of the city centre big billboards loom up. Coca-Cola. Shell. BHP. Ugly faces on stilts. We can see them through the window.

'Tomorrow,' Natalya is saying, 'tomorrow Vitaly has to see his lawyer. He has to plead "not guilty", or we can't build a case.'

I nod slowly. 'I think Vitaly wants to tell the truth,' I say. I put my palms flat on the table. 'I don't think he cares, now. Not about the trial, not about anything. Except Staciya.'

'Fuck, Fiona—I care. He's part of my family. I love my family. It's the only one I've got. Did he tell you that this afternoon? That he doesn't care. . .if he goes to gaol? Jesus Christ. This is all because of the silver budgie Zionist, bloody Hawkie. Bob Hawke. Shit.'

'Natalya, don't say that. Please don't say that.'

I am pleading. My words sound small and weak. My sister is starting to hate. My sister. My sister who has never hated anything.

I remember her giving me the hiding of my life when, as a ten-year-old, I pointed at some drunken Aborigines in Musgrave Park, and giggled. 'Don't laugh,' she yelled. 'It's not funny. They can't help it. It's Christmas,' she said. 'It's all they have.'

Christmas is coming around again, and David Jones is busy. 'Only twenty-two shopping days until Christmas,' a sign outside proclaims.

'I hope they have a lousy Christmas,' Natalya grumbles. 'I hope Santa shits on them.'

'They don't have Christmas,' I say.

THE LAWYER'S face is red and his hands tremble. His distinguished silver hair is tousled, and his tie is loose. He does not look commanding at all. He has a small white scar above his right eye; it throbs, turning purple as we watch. He is standing before his desk, papers in hand, facing Vitaly and Staciya; they are seated around his mahogany desk like the members of a coven. I stand at the back of the room, listening, idly twisting the component parts of a Rubik's cube in my hands. Staciya does not want me there, and periodically she barks at Vitaly in Ukrainian. He shrugs his shoulders, and smiles at her. The lawyer takes a step forward.

We are seeing the lawyer—a good lawyer who Vitaly would not normally be able to afford—because the Australian government believes in justice and in certain cases provides legal aid. The lawyer is opposed to war crimes trials, he has principles, ideals. Cathe calls him a 'labor lawyer'. His politics are displayed on stickers on the filing cabinet behind him. 'If you think the system's working, ask someone who isn't.' 'One nuclear bomb can ruin your whole day.' 'Agitate-Educate-Organise.' This upsets Staciya. It makes her feel like she is accepting charity. She sits in the lawyer's comfortable leather armchair, bareheaded, twisting her scarf in her fingers. The lawyer is shaking his head. These people, these people, they are difficult to understand.

'They have no evidence. The charges may be dropped. But I have not had any word.' He breathes hard, rasping. 'It must be hard for you.'

'They will have their show trial.'

'They got nothing from Polyukhovich, Mr. Kovalenko. That was truly a show trial, and it made them look very silly indeed.'

'He was Byelorussian, not Ukrainian. They hate us more.'

'Mr. Kovalenko, this is Australia. Telling the difference between various ethnic groups is not our forte.'

'They hate us. You do not understand.'

'Do you hate them?'

'I stopped for a long while, but now it starts again. In here. In my soul.' He prods his chest. 'In here.'

The lawyer moves behind his desk and sits down, very slowly, pressing down with his knuckles on the shiny desk top. He breathes in deeply, pursing his lips. His fist contracts around the biro he is holding. The brittle plastic shatters. Bright-blue ink and bright, cherry-red blood mingle on the leather inlay.

I SORT THE transcriptions into three piles. Next to my inkwell is a folder marked 'Vitaly' in thick black felt pen. On the floor is another, similar folder, marked 'Dad'. In my hands four fat spiral pads hold Kateryna's testimony. I label a folder with her name, slide the notebooks into it. Pinned to my noticeboard is a wartime photograph of Vitaly with Magda, the Polish woman he married. They stare blankly out of the past at me. She has a pretty face. Since liberation in 1989, she and Vitaly have started writing to each other. Their letters are crazily illiterate. Even with my poor Ukrainian, I can read them. Staciya does not care. Vitaly has learnt that his son is an agronomist with the new Wałesa government. He is proud, but the polaroid snaps of the boy mean little to him. It is the woman, and her round, innocent face, that he remembers. Beside the photo, in chronological order, newspaper clippings about the war crimes trials are tacked up, yellowing at the corners, curling now. I have dated them, and the ink has faded; it is grey and insipid. A cartoon that pokes fun at both Marxism and the Queensland Police sits in the centre of the war crimes clippings. It's a good cartoon.

Post-it notes flutter below the cartoon. A quotation from Stalin. . .'I want their wings broken'. The phone number of the Greenpeace Brisbane office. The date of an impending visit by the *Rainbow Warrior.* Well below Stalin's words, the most recent Amnesty International bulletin is propped against the bedroom wall. It's too heavy to pin to the noticeboard. There is a book of tickets that I've yet to sell for a Greenpeace raffle at my elbow. An appeal from the Labor Party for scrutineers on polling day falls on the floor as I sit up. My CDs are piled on top of my CD player. I haven't had time to put them away. My desk, I once said, is a mirror in which all my various political causes are reflected. I look at the letter from the ALP on the floor. These trials are ruling my desk.

My light blazes out onto the dark street, defiantly. One night, such as this, I went outside to see what the house looked like, with only one window filled with light. Sickly yellow beams illuminated the rockery. I suck the nib of my pen. My tongue must be black by now. I dip it in the ink, poise it above the blank paper before me. Vitaly goes to Treblinka, I write, and underline it. <u>Vitaly goes to Treblinka</u>. It has permanence, now. I must own it. I look at it, grimly going about my task.

Have I found the past? I write. Was it different from or more complicated than the past I know and understand? Is it worth telling others about this past? I am disturbed by a knock on the door. 'Enter!' I call, my voice muffled by the amount of paper scattered everywhere.

Cathe steps softly into the room and sits on my bed. 'Fiona,' she says, 'your mother is on the phone. It sounds urgent.' I stumble into the lounge.

'Fiona love, it's Mum here. Your uncle's had a stroke. He's in intensive care at Southport Hospital. He can talk OK, but he can't move his legs. You've got to get down here fast, love. Quick as you can.'

'Quick as I can, Mum.'

I wonder, as I make another trip to the Gold Coast, if it is worry about the trial that has caused Vitaly's stroke. Or if it is just general stress and old age. He frets now, dodders around the house unable to undertake normal household chores; his yard crumbles around him. I speed down the freeway; it is pretty at night. The twinkling lights of Southbank are comforting. 'Comfort, comfort, all my people, with the comfort of my word. . .' What's that? Hymn I learnt at school. I sing the melody out loud. A new BMW passes me, its driver looking in my direction with a perturbed expression on her face. I grin at her, gamely. A truck honks me from behind, then honks again as he overtakes. 'Trucker-fucker', I hiss to myself.

I could drive like this forever, slide all the way down the eastern seaboard to Melbourne, even Adelaide. But now, I don't want to go to Adelaide. Not if I can help it. A horrible thought occurs to me. Another stroke will rob the trials of their victim. I push the thought to one side, and concentrate. Another stroke. . .

UKRAINIAN children gather outside the schoolyard in the Colonia collective two miles from the village. Clean Russian children play in the school; therefore it occupies Ukrainian dreams. The Ukrainians sit outside and wait for the smallest Russian children to come out and play so that they can steal their lunches. Blood sausage and tasty oatcakes. Sandwiches cut into four tidy squares. They beat the plump children of the revolution, these incautious Russian colonists, take their food and flee. The little Russians look at the big, dirty, hollow-cheeked adolescents who come after them with such unbridled fury and start to cry. But today the NKVD have ringed the school with soldiers and machine-guns, and the Ukrainians go home empty-stomached. Spite, mean-spirited and angry. The children complain to their parents: help us. There is not enough to feed us. Why do they hate us?

WHEN VITALY was eight years old, the NKVD came to the town of Khmel'nik to enforce Comrade Kaganovich's and Comrade Stalin's collectivisation order. They had started the process earlier, but the Great Leader warned against the dangers of 'dizziness from success', and Khmel'nik was untouched. But this time, they came and took Ivan Bosko's farm, the largest and most prosperous farm in the district, and created the nucleus of the new kolkhoz. They killed Bosko and his family, and the drunken kommissar and his doctor wife moved into the now empty house.

We can't meet these quotas.

Yes you can. Turn your land over to the kolkhoz and farm to build socialism! The quotas are only half there than what they are on private land!

Very well, we shall go.

One day Vitaly came home from the school, after a stealing expedition, to see that his home was no longer occupied by his parents. A poster of Kaganovich and Stalin was pasted to the wall facing the road, and a uniformed NKVD man sat on the porch. Vitaly sprinted along the dirt path that led to the front steps. The communist did not move.

'Where's my mummy?'

'Who are you?'

'Vitaly Kovalenko. I live here with my sister and my brother and mummy and daddy and Bohdan my dog.'

'You mean this?' The NKVD man held up the skinned carcass of a small mongrel dog. Vitaly noticed that the bayonet on the man's rifle was bloody. His face crumpled, and the house tipped weirdly on its side, distorted through his tears and narrowed eyes. The NKVD man stood up and walked slowly down the steps.

'What have you got in your hand?' Vitaly surrendered the sandwiches and apple he had stolen from a crying Russian four-year-old. 'You worthless scum! Stealing from the true Children of the Revolution!'

He delivered a devastating jackbooted kick to Vitaly's arse, propelling him along the new, freshly graded road before the kolkhoz gates with yells and fists. Behind the ornate iron gate topped with the hammer and sickle, Vitaly saw his parents standing, belongings collected in a pathetic heap behind them. His mother cried. She held a large ikon of St George in her hands. His little sister hid her head behind it, clutching her mother's skirts. His father held Evheny in his arms. Evheny turned his red, tear-streaked face away when he saw the NKVD man, burying it in his father's embroidered shirt.

'Now get in there, Ukrainian shit.' He pushed Vitaly towards his parents. He looked up, glaring at Fyodor Kovalenko and his dusty, frightened family. 'You're lucky I didn't have you deported as a kulak. Living like a fucking baron in that house.'

'It is my house, which I built with my own hands.'

The NKVD man was drunk. He reeled sloppily forwards, wagging his finger in front of Fyodor's nose. '*Fucking* bourgeois nationalist. I'll give you Ukraine. Ha. Fuck you.' He turned to leave.

Fyodor looked down, his grey eyes hard and unmoved. 'Tell me one thing.' The NKVD man wheeled, wobbling unsteadily. 'What?'

'Are you a Jew, like your master Kaganovich?'

'I am a Bolshevik. My race is irrelevant.' He stumbled away.

He yelled 'I'll have you all deported, all of you, every last one.'

Vitaly did not come to appreciate the new, draughty house to which his family had been sent, and soon the quotas on the collective were as high as those on private land. Eventually, guards were posted around the Russian colonists' school, and that food source was blocked. Then Kaganovich ordered the destruction of all ikons in the Ukraine, and the local supply was burnt on a big bonfire in the largest and nicest open space in the middle of the collective. Vitaly and his father brought all the ikons in their house to the fire except one, which they hid. The next day, Vitaly came home from the fields where he now worked to find small pieces of Saint George scattered around his mother's vegetable garden. The communists had found it and destroyed it. Later, he found a large, runny human shit where it had been hidden. He bent down, scrabbling to collect the pieces of skewered saint. 'Here's Saint George's head! Here's his buckler, here's the front end of the horse. . .and there's some of the dragon!' He held the pieces in childish, grubby hands. He could never put Saint George back together again. He cried, clutching the shattered ikon to his chest. 'Saint George,' he prayed, 'I know I'm a naughty boy, I had a dirty dream about that girl again, but please don't let this happen to us. Please Saint George, save us.'

We can't meet these quotas. I thought you said it would be better on the collective.

But, comrade, you must make them, for Comrade Stalin and for socialism!

But we are already hungry. Another harvest like the last and we will starve.

That is really too bad. You are all kulaks and revisionist nationalists anyway.

I do not understand those big words.

That, comrade, is because you are a stupid Ukrainian.

EACH YEAR the wheat gets shorter, and each year the communists take more of the harvest. They post guard towers around the collective and shoot peasants caught gleaning around the perimeter of the fields. They take the seed for next year's crop and kill a few more mature men for being kulaks. With the arrest and detention of Fyodor Kovalenko, there are no more adult men left on the collective. The NKVD come and chain women and boys together, and driving them on with whips, yell 'Work, you bastards, work!' over their bent backs. The fertiliser runs into the stream and makes its waters undrinkable. People are so hungry that they eat their farm animals and then corpse-meat. 'Look', says the doctor, 'these savages are cannibals.' The kommissar says nothing, pushing away his amply loaded plate. He drinks. He grows thin like his people.

The land is rich and fruitful, the grass grows thick and matted. The rain comes, the wheat and the grass grow, well-watered plains shine gold under an iridescent clear sky. The NKVD and their tractors and their superphosphates come. When the people do not understand the new methods, the NKVD sow the fields with salt. The land is barren, the grass does not grow. Do not walk on the land with bare feet, it cuts. Do not walk on the land. The peasants scratch at the ungrateful earth with blunt mattocks. Blood runs in the soil.

The NKVD dynamite the village church. It is a stone and wood church, so the masonry and timber flies high and wide, leaving a ragged and satisfying circle. The NKVD pour kerosene over the Bible, burn it dramatically leaf by leaf before the entire village. After they leave, the people return to the stone circle, thin like shadows. They pray, but are too weak and sick to sing. One of the walls is still more or less intact. During the night someone steals some paint from the party stores, and in the morning the kommissar wakes to find the word 'freedom' painted on the ruined wall with bold red letters. It is misspelt, but it still goads him. *Freedom*.

Each Friday, the NKVD come and collect the dead, frozen bodies, and Vitaly watches as the body of his baby brother is thrown on the back of a truck. He stands by the side of the road in clothes that once belonged to his father, and they flap and flutter in the wind.

The NKVD man remembers Vitaly because Vitaly stole from the true children of the revolution. Comrade Zhivkov, who used to be Comrade Rosendjuft but has rejected his Jewish name, gives the boy hell at the new compulsory political education classes. He calls him out because he doesn't know the answers, kicks him when he cries, locks him in the cupboard when he answers back. Vitaly is the biggest boy in the class, the one most likely to stand up, the one with his head still full of Cossack dreams and songs, the one who still thinks he owns this country; this clean, spare, pretty country.

VITALY: What I remember most is the way they came for our land, our animals, our people. Just poor folk, who had nothing before the revolution and nothing after it, either.

We moved onto the collective, but they didn't give us anything to live in. If you complained they blacklisted the whole collective, and you starved real quick, instead of real slow. This is what happened to us, in my home village. We didn't make our quota, so they black-listed us.

Because they gave us nothing to live in, people pinched scrap wood and metal from the kommissar's rubbish heap. We also made mud bricks from the wheat stubble that had been ploughed in by the NKVD. I think Vanya the kommissar turned a blind eye to the stealing from his rubbish dump, but if you got caught by his wife you were shot.

Soon we had quite a good shantytown, but it wasn't so good if it rained or it snowed, which was most of the time, because it leaked. Then we didn't make our quota. The quota was so high, it was amazing. I never saw an acre of land produce as much as they said it would. First they sent brigades to clean out our stores of grain. But it wasn't anywhere near the quota. So they broke into our shanties and took anything we had stored away. Then they shut the party store, and blew up the windmill. Finally they bulldozed the shanties and we had nothing to live in. Signs were put up in Khmel'nik and Evheny told me they said that no party store was to serve anyone from Kolkhoz 28.

My cousin Lara, she went to Khmel'nik to beg. I went with her. She begged next to the people in the bread queue. No one had anything to give, they were all starving as well. Finally she got to the storekeeper, a Russian colonist. She begged at him. He said she was too lazy to work on the farm. He yelled at her, and hit her hand with the knife. Luckily it was blunt. Lara fell down and lost the crumb of bread she had in one hand. Then the storekeeper came out from behind the stall and kicked her and kicked her, all the while yelling at her to get up, go home, and work.

People in the queue started to cry, and two men pulled her away from the Russian. He said we are soft, and don't want to work for socialism. He said we are enemies of the people. Lara finally came and took my hand. She said it is no good. We must just wait and suffer, like it say in the Bible.

In the meantime I got so skinny you could count all my ribs, and my elbows stuck out like knots in cotton.

IT IS 1933. The village starves. The women's menstrual periods stop from fear and hunger. The NKVD come each night in their black cars. Wear three sets of underwear, even in summer. Keep a coat and hat beside your bed. They will take us all.

It is 1935. The communists decide to leave some grain in Ukraine for the Ukrainians. No one knows why: they just do it. The boy is fourteen. The girl in the dirty dream is Ulrike Uhrman, the daughter of the town's only Volksdeutsche. She comes from Gorky. Her mother is Russian. Her father was sent to do the collective's bookkeeping. It is just as well, the villagers say. His soft hands are useless in the fields.

It is 1938. Vitaly is seventeen. Ulrike is fifteen. She reads and writes, and she says she likes him. He looks over her shoulder, wonder and innocence and desire chasing each other across his face. She lets him kiss her in the evenings after work. She admires him as she watches him sluice himself off under the collective's pump. *Look at Vitaly Fyodorovich. . .isn't he handsome?* Her father does not care, she says. He has a sister, her aunt, in the Party in Moscow. Her aunt says that Christian morality is an agent of capitalist repression. Vitaly does not understand her words. She speaks them but also does not understand. She has vixen-green eyes and black hair, her breasts lie round and heavy under her smock. Comrade Zhivkov says 'You better stay away from that Vitaly Fyodorovich. Blood runs with blood. His father helped the counter-revolutionary scum. Ukrainians—stay away from them. You steer clear of Vitaly Fyodorovich.'

It is 1939. It is Lenin's birthday. The collective does not starve now. It goes hungry occasionally, but people do not starve. The NKVD come and take people still, but not too often. Vitaly even obtains an ikon, a beautiful glowing head of Christ. He lights a tallow candle before it each night at bedtime. He shows this carbon-stained ikon to Ulrike, swearing her to secrecy. She kisses his beautiful face, laughs at the shining light in his tinted-blue eyes. She does not see the hate underneath the land, or how the land runs into his feet. The communists have maimed the land, so the boy is also maimed. He laughs and he is beautiful, and she loves him. She ignores Comrade Zhivkov. She tells people that he is an ugly Jew and no woman will touch him, and that's his problem. 'Lenin's birthday,' she says. 'We have a good time then, ay Vitaly?'

LENIN'S birthday meant a day off, and, for once, no one worried. Even the communist killjoys could be seen smiling and laughing and drinking. It was like Christmas used to be, in The Good Old Days. The whole village would parade in new red scarves and white shirts sent from Kiev or Moscow before the kommissar and his mean Dr Judit. The Kommissar would obtain as much nice food as possible, and give sweets to the children who showed the most 'socialist spirit', even though his wife complained. 'Eat, sleep, work, breed,' she said to him once. 'That's all these people want.' 'Ah, yes,' he almost answered, 'and when they die, they want to go to heaven.' But it was bad form to love his own people, or to confess that, for him, heaven sounded inviting and secure.

The parade finished mid-morning, which then left a long, delicious day of freedom. Ulrike came to Vitaly's house before the parade, in the sharp, cool, slanting light of early morning. Natasha Kovalenko saw them kissing greedily through the open shutters, his hands buried in her clothes. Natasha smiled warmly. Things were happening again in Ukraine, at last.

AFTER THE parade. Mirochnik's barn. Yes. Stop for now, you're messing up my clothes. Soon. Love you. Love you. He stands grimly all through the parade, fiercely reciting the words to the 'Internationale', Stalin and Lenin's real names, and the cities of the Soviet Union, to prevent his erection from becoming resoundingly public. He sees bruised Lara grinning vacantly and beaten Nikolai with his head down. Evheny is selected to read a passage from Marx, the kommissar's wife thinking it beneath her dignity to read to 'the Breeders'. Evheny looks funny, the great red tome threatening to tumble from his straining hands to the platform below as he speaks. Vitaly sees Ulrike win some sweets for demonstrating great 'socialist spirit', and wonders how she does it. She winks at him during the kommissar's long and boring and drunken speech, 'together we are building socialism' then is the first to sprint away when the parade is dismissed. Affecting non-chalance, he follows, hands in pockets. His beautiful old mother is watching, and smiling at him.

When he reaches the barn, Ulrike is seated on the floor, her blouse undone, her red scarf tied fetchingly in her hair. She shows her breasts, lifting them gently with stiff fingers. He kneels before her. 'I've got a sweet for you', she says. She holds it gently between her lips. He reaches out to take it with his fingers, but she draws his face towards hers with a firm grip. He takes the sweet with his own lips. The taste is urgently pleasant, and he sucks her lips and her candy together. He slides her blouse off her shoulders, and cups the soft mounds of her breasts in his hands. She helps him; her clothes are strewn all over the floor of the barn, and her hair is tangled with straw. He has some trouble getting his pants down, finally succeeds, then explores between her legs with his fingers. She stiffens for a moment, and he thinks he has hurt her, but she holds his hand in place. 'There. Put it in there. That's nice.' She can see his breath in the cold, clear air. She unbuttons his thick shirt with one hand and guides him in with the other, hooking her legs over his back. The awk-wardness of his body begins to ease. She says, 'Hold me tight, I'm cold.' He comes immediately, but then takes longer the second time, staying inside her. 'Ooo, you're nice,' she keeps saying, her hands stroking the soft, blond hair on his back.

Mirochnik, the old hoary peasant, is aware that his barn—
or what was formerly his barn and now belongs to Kolkhoz
28—is the rendezvous where all sorts of illicit activities are
undertaken. In the past, before collectivisation, he would have
maintained that such activities were dirty and cheap, that the
young couple should wait for the marriage night when the
whole village would gather around the groom's house making
a racket with kitchen utensils, singing and dancing up a storm.
When he hears a woman's voice uttering a sharp cry of
pleasure, he nods to himself and understands. There is a fresh
painting of Stalin on the side of the barn, a giant face fringed
with red flags. Taking care to make sure that no one is looking,
he kicks a cow shit still soft in the centre towards the painting,
striking Comrade Stalin in the mouth. The shit fans out
asymmetrically, like the fluid beside an overturned inkpot,
obliterating the dictator's lips and making his moustache
absurdly lopsided.

They resolve to marry, and his mother is pleased. Even
though there is no church, there are still weddings, with lots
of vodka and sweets and fancy bread. The whole village
celebrating. Tables laid out with white cloth. The former priest
sneaking a few surreptitious blessings to the young lovers
over a glass. Even the Kommissar would come. Ulrike now
wears a thin gold band on one finger, to show that she is
taken. The band once belonged to Natasha. Natasha stopped
wearing it when she no longer had a husband. 'Take it. Let it
give you joy.' To Vitaly she says, 'Go and lie with her. There
is little else for you now.' Ulrike admires it in the candlelight
before Vitaly's beautiful ikon, turning her hand about and
around. She strokes Vitaly's head, pushes his yellow hair
away from his eyes. He has a little blond moustache, a soft,
golden beard. They tickle her as he kisses her breasts.

But the Volksdeutsche are taken, not just from Khmel'nik
but from the collectives as well, and the big black NKVD car
comes to the farms, generating mixed awe and dread. *We must*

arrest these revisionist enemies of the people! The members of the Uhrman family—even the Russian wife and mother—are bundled into the back seat. The Jewish NKVD man, Zhivkov/Rosendjuft, in charge of the collectivisation of some years earlier, drives the car. Later Natasha says, 'So much for the aunt in the Party.'

Vitaly is engaged in the task of ploughing legumes into the field beside the road that leads through the collective when he sees this. He abandons the horse-drawn plough to its fate and chases the car; its spinning wheels cover him with mud. 'Bring her back,' he yells, 'I'm going to marry her. Bring her back, I love her.' He kneels in the street, as though praying. First he cries. Hot, salty tears. A candle of snot hangs pendulously from the base of his nose. He pulls it away. Then he dreams. Dreams how he can kill. Gently, Mirochnik the farmer, after slowly and stiffly striding to the centre of the road, pulls the sobbing boy to his feet. 'Do not forget her,' he says. 'Do not forget this.'

THE BLOND, tanned young man sitting in the back of a German SS lorry with forty comrades looks out onto the devastated countryside. Briefly he remembers a bloodied scythe rising above the heads of wheat in his home village, hears its hacking blows as they are delivered to the body of some yesterday powerful communist kommissar.

He does not know the truth: Kaganovich only kept his power because he was shorter than Stalin, a good two inches shorter. Vitaly thinks that he kept his power through Jewish cunning. He does not know that no one is cunning enough to outsmart Comrade Stalin, and that Comrade Kaganovich enjoyed a measure of authority only because it suited Comrade Stalin for him to do so.

Kaganovich's reward for his extraordinary loyalty was to be posted to the Ukraine, land of giants. Oh, how it irked him that these people were taller than he! So he wanted power. Power over this sullen race that refused to part with its fields.

Vitaly also feels power himself. He is free. Free to drink himself into a legless happiness. Free to kill his enemies, the killers of his people. Free to fuck the peasant girls who believe in his divinity because he has such a fine black uniform. And many feel as he does.

He is accompanied by many. In Kiev, Voronikov's mother starved to death, leaving her boy pawing at her grey hand as it hung over the side of the copper bath. In Vinnitsa, Nikolai saw NKVD deport his parents as kulaks, and lost his uncle for sabotage on the collective. In Ulan Erge, the Buddhist temple was burnt down, and the boy Shura was led out to the front of the classroom in the new 'Communist Party School of Kalmykia' to scratch out the word 'family' written in large Cyrillic letters on the blackboard, while his classmates were forced to applaud. The Headman was dead. The communists had sawed his arms off the night before. The Russians hated the yellow people of his country. They forbade the speaking of Mongolian, the use of script. The boy cried as he crossed out the word. There was no music, even among this singing race, to describe these things.

Vitaly clutches the rifle he has learned to fire to his chest. He heads for service in the inner circles of Hell. Tomorrow, he will arrive in Treblinka.

Through the front gate, a carved, scalloped edifice, there is a riot going on. The air is full of bugs, crawling all over the new arrivals and up their nostrils. Someone yells 'About time they got here from Warsaw' and throws his hands above his head, a gesture at once angry and placatory. Dr Eberl is looking out of his office window; he has a fine young face. Liszt is playing through the loudspeakers scattered around the compound. Dr Eberl conducts an imaginary orchestra with a pearl baton that his wife gave him last Christmas. There are too many deportees to be gassed. He points his baton at the

German in charge of the Warsaw Ghetto Ukrainians. 'To the sorting area. There's a job there for them that I need done. At once!'

There, because the gas chambers have broken down for the nth time that month, the entire transport is to be shot. As the thunder of rifles and machine-guns commences, Dr Eberl relents and plays some Wagner—something from *Tristan und Isolde*—to appease his deputy. 'About time you stopped playing that bloody Hungarian all the time.'

THE SS placed the Ukrainians in a barracks of their own, and supplied them with ample food and vodka. Eberl, the witty and clever Kommandant, a graduate of Vienna University, encouraged the singing of those 'borrowed' from Warsaw to assist with security. Soon, every morning, the killing fields rang with lively peasant aubades. The separateness of the Ukrainians and their German overlords was important: the Master Race could not be seen to be living too closely with such savages. 'If we keep them happy,' he told his close friend Willie, 'then they will finish this wicked and necessary task all by themselves.'

Later that first week, during a pause between transports, Vitaly saw a beautiful young man in a Waffen SS uniform talking with Dr Eberl on his landing. The young man listened seriously to the things Dr Eberl said. 'Resoluteness! The group that chooses to be led by a *hero!* This is what matters!' Vitaly heard Eberl say loudly, while the lovely young man nodded. Vitaly stopped to admire the visitor. His hair was so shiny and silver, his eyes such portals of light, that Vitaly felt sure that he must be perfect. Although Eberl seemed handsome enough, and some of Vitaly's fellow Ukrainians had fine hair and eyes, the beauty of the man seemed improbable in this place.

The young man stopped nodding, and said, 'In my paper for Dr Martin, I argued that authenticity must be attained in

the face of technologisation. And Martin argues that resoluteness and authenticity are inextricably linked.' He made small,
neat, chopping motions with his hands as he spoke. Eberl had
been drawing furiously on his pipe and rubbing his hands
together the whole time that the young man was speaking,
when he glanced downwards from his vantage point and
spotted Vitaly staring at them. He stood up and glowered
over the balustrade. 'Piss off back to the shooting pits, Ukrainian savage. The mind of Martin Heidegger is far too fine for
the likes of you.' Vitaly saluted smartly and apologised, first
to the Kommandant, and then to the beautiful stranger. The
young man nodded his perfect head. 'No hard feelings,' he
said, softly. 'I am taking up far too much of the Herr
Kommandant's time with my endless speculations, but nonetheless, I believe it's important that. . .'

THROUGH the gate, down the road, hunting, hunting escapees.
Too much work, not enough security. Eberl wants to set new
targets. Eberl is competing with Herr Hoess in Auschwitz. He
is not aware that Herr Hoess holds a technological advantage:
more efficient gas. There are Polish villages around the camp.
The Jews take refuge in them.

'How do you find Jews in here, ay? I don't speak Polish.'
'Simple. Give the Poles a hundred złoty and enough vodka
to last 'em until Christmas. Then they give us the Jews. It
doesn't always work. The woods are full of *Armia Krajowa*,
Polish partisans. But it works well enough to keep the Germans happy.'

The Poles queue next to the Nazi lorry. Vitaly and Shura
pass bottles and money to these eager helpers. Finally the
Poles turn home, some of them already staggering drunkenly.
Vitaly looks at the three captured Jews, two men and one
woman.

Vitaly asks, 'What do we do with them?'

Shura answers, 'Eberl says we have to shoot them.'

'Couldn't we just let them go?'

'Not really. The Germans say they are diseased.'

THE POLISH residents of the Treblinka district were not particularly resentful of this foreign invasion, although some of the yellow-skinned Kazakhs and Kalmyks in the garrison took a little time to assimilate. The peasants from the Ukraine, the Poles appreciated, paid good money for their drink and soon attracted prostitutes and business from Małkinia and Warsaw, which meant money for the town. *It doesn't matter what colour it is, if it spends money, so much the better.* The Ukrainians were handsome, and friendly enough, and as nearly everyone in Treblinka village was related, benefit for one villager meant benefit for the many.

Vitaly found himself a rich man since he received German wage rates and was in the position to loot as he liked from the incoming transports of Jews. His freedom was remarkable, indeed. He could buy whatever pleased him, do whatever he found amusing. He visited the city of Warsaw, free now to veer away from the ghetto, his former place of employment, and he saw for the first time a beautiful city with street lamps and taxicabs and trolley cars. He gazed with wonder through lighted shop windows, his nose crawling like a snail on the glass as the busy Poles around him went to and from their places of occupation, busy because, for all its calm and solidity, theirs was a city under siege.

THE MASTER Race prided itself on its efficiency. It did not like its establishments administered in such a shoddy fashion. Eberl, who seemed to think he was the grand duke of some ghastly medieval estate, was unceremoniously sacked. The official reason given was 'sexual deviance'. Vitaly saw him on the final day of his command, talking with the silver-haired young man again. He seemed to be complaining. The young man had a fat pile of books bound with a leather strap tucked under his arm. Beside him was a girl—no more than a teen-ager—with flowing strawberry-coloured hair. The girl was very pretty, wearing a flat-bellied skirt and long cape. She stared at Eberl. Her pout registered boredom. Eberl said, 'Well, Willie, this is it.' Silver Willie shook his head, sadly. Extra trucks were needed to transport Eberl's library from the camp. Willie was seeing that they were loaded properly. He waved his arms energetically at the two youthful Ukrainians loading the trucks. 'No, you idiot, empiricism over there. How dare you put John Stuart Mill beside Nietzsche!'

So Eberl and his Liszt records, assorted university degrees, capacity for philosophical speculation, women's clothes and fierce competitive spirit were exchanged for Herr Stangl's stolidly middle-class organisational skills: he had run a foot-ball club, a school P&C and a Veteran's Society. He had a complete edition of Shakespeare and a complete edition of Goethe. This was food enough for his mind. He said, 'Leave these University queers alone for a month and look what they do.' He respected order, ritual, piety. The cities of Poland with their prominent churches reminded him of his childhood. His tuition by the Dominicans. *Domini canes*: the Hounds of God.

Herr Stangl stopped transports altogether for a brief dura-tion, and attempted to control the rampant alcoholism of his staff. 'God these Ukrainians can stick it away. I've never seen anything like it.' He had some new gas chambers built, larger, more efficient, prettier. The steps were embellished with potted geraniums. The entrance was covered by a synagogue's ceremonial curtain. On it were written the words 'This is the Gateway to God. Righteous Men will pass through.' There was a gable decorated with a large Star of David. There was even a glass porthole you could look through to see how things were going.

Stangl accepted one recommendation of Eberl's, and appointed clever Karol Rohozin, who could read Polish and German, as commander of the Ukrainian garrison. Stangl set up the lie of the *Lazarett*, a burning pit disguised as a field hospital, within which those too sick to run to the gas chambers would be shot by a bored Ukrainian sentry after being duped outside by a fluttering Red Cross flag. Stangl controlled the looting carried out by the Ukrainian garrison, and arranged proper rosters. He set up a camp orchestra and choir, and played Christmas carols over the loudspeakers during the festive season. Stangl also, in letters home, despite the lack of linguistic resemblance between the British Raj and the Third Reich, referred to the Ukrainians as 'native troops'. Thus, they became, fairly rapidly, the sepoys, the Askaris, of the Nazi Empire. Expendable, obedient, loyal and dependably heartless. They did not try, as yet, to throw out their foreign masters, or place them in a black hole in the ground. It was only later, when those still in the villages realised that the Nazis had no plans for them as people (they were too useful as savages), that they began to fight back. *Then* they became partisans. But they had two battles to fight: one against the communists, and one against the Nazis. They also lost.

THERE ARE only seventeen Germans in the camp, and one hundred and twenty Ukrainians. There are Polish and Ukrainian women who also live on the premises, cooking and washing for their compatriots in labour. There are also nine hundred prisoners. They are carpenters and doctors, jewellers and watchmakers. They sort the clothes and valuables of the dead, they regularly bribe the Ukrainian guards with the valuables they steal in order to save their lives, and they are not fed starvation rations, because their work is 'important'. Everyone else who comes to this centre for resettlement and re-education is gassed.

From among the Germans, Kiwe is in charge of the *Lazarett*, Sidow the brush-collecting detail (it is vital that the whole place is surrounded by scented pine brush) and Franz the sorting yard. Franz has a pet Saint Bernard, Barri, which has taken a liking to Vitaly, and Barri follows Vitaly around the compound when he is off duty, simpering. Barri also kills people at Franz's command, by tearing out their throats. But there is also a human dog in the camp, Ivan the Terrible, who co-administers the gas chambers with Nikolai Manchuk. Not a hunchback, but worthy of comparison with Quasimodo for his fury.

Stangl the *Herr Kommandant* is seldom seen; he is not an educated man, like the previous incumbent. Rumours persist about what he *does* in there. His musical taste is appalling. Fortunately, he leaves the singing to the Ukrainians and the instrumentations to the Jewish orchestra. When they play, the people in the nearby villages hear sweet music pouring forth from what they know is a human abattoir. The guards sing and dance, even the prisoners sing as they march hither and thither. Each week a concert is held in the Tailor Shop, and there is dancing and singing. The Kommandant is a tidy man. Each day two different Ukrainians are rostered to stand beneath the trees on his grounds and catch the leaves *before* they fall to earth. Nothing so vulgar as a piece of rubbish in sight.

VITALY, like most of the garrison, avoids the *Lazarett* detail. It makes him feel sick. He thought he would be fighting Bolshevism. He sits beside the pit on a canvas chair, his rifle perched on one knee, waiting for the hour's quota of victims to be escorted past the Red Cross flag and through the gate. Depending on the number of victims, he will do the shooting alone or enlist the assistance of the escort—usually three men. Sometimes Ivan M. is one of these guards. He is a corporal, and he has Vitaly throw infants in the air so that he may attempt to catch them on his bayonet. One of the German overseers has a phrase—'long pig'—something to do with the South Sea Islanders, which he uses near the shooting pit when Ivan M. is there. Vitaly does not like it. It sounds bad. The German cackles. Ivan's swift movements with the bayonet make 'whooshing' sounds. The sleeves of his uniform—long on him because he is very young—become soaked. The bodies in the fire make crackling, roasting sounds, and sometimes new visitors to the *Lazarett* throw up before undertaking their shooting tasks. Shura did this, then recovered sufficiently to remind Ivan that a rifle that filthy must take no small amount of cleaning. Vitaly is glad that the *Lazarett* roster only lasts for one week. But he is well paid. He has a photo of himself taken in Warsaw, in a proper professional studio. He is handsome, his blond hair sleek like a shiny cap on his head. His uniform fits him better, now: he has filled out and grown another inch. Six feet six. It has a nice ring to it. He comes stalking down the dusty streets of the town near the camp, heading for the house of the old, bent peasant Sławek Juskowiak who sells good quality Polish vodka, under a soft, black summer sky. It is in this state of lordly power—rich, handsome and free— that he meets Magda Juskowiak.

THE HOUSE of Sławek Juskowiak had only three rooms, large rooms with whitewashed walls and slate floors. Sławek and his wife Maria slept in one room, with Magda and Brunek, the oldest of the children still at home, occupying the space at the foot of the paternal bed on hewn wooden bunks. On the very coldest days, the best milk cow would also share this room with Sławek and Maria. Four more children occupied the next room, sleeping on matting and burlap sacks, their ages ranging, stair-step, from three to eleven. There was Nowak, little and bright-eyed, the youngest boy, beloved of

Maria Juskowiak. Then Leokadja, a blond and pretty girl, not quite old enough to fetch water from the pump in the yard. Then Anna, who was old enough, and undertook this task each morning and evening. Finally, Piotr, who, along with thirteen-year-old Brunek, looked after the few cows with his father, and brought the hay in, when the time was right, and the potatoes, when the time was right, and married, also when the time was right.

The third room was kitchen and shop both: a wooden partition at the rear kept the actual living space of the family hidden. Sławek and Magda and Brunek served vodka through its opened shutters to thirsty workers, farmers and Ukrainians, underneath a handsome gilt ikon of the Virgin, donated by one of the Ukrainians, a very religious farmboy, Berik Houmenko. Maria cooked behind these shutters, over a little peat stove, using lard and meat that the Ukrainians brought from the camp, her round, rutted face set in concentration. In the kitchen was a large wooden table, its top worn shiny smooth by the generations of Juskowiaks who had sat around it to eat. Maria served crispy savoury sausage to eager patrons, and always saved some of the meat for her brood. The Ukrainians did not mind that Sławek charged them three times as much as the locals for drink. The peasants were poor, and Ukrainians could always obtain liquor from the camp: even though it was inferior to Juskowiak's brew, it had the same effect. 'You know old Juskowiak,' said Tadek the butcher, 'he's going to be a rich man!' All the villagers could remember how the Juskowiak's poor land-holding had killed Sławek's father. Jan always worked very hard to make his land productive, frequently labouring fourteen hours a day. As a result of this he died pushing the plough. The horse returned to the house by a roundabout route, dragging the plough lopsidedly behind. Sławek found his father's body stretched out face down in the furrow. He arranged a big wake, then began to work the land himself.

Sometimes the Ukrainians brought the inferior camp vodka with them, in bottles, and would sit in the dirt, on the steps, chit-chattering and drinking. Until, in their cups, they would fall asleep. Often, Anna sought the help of her father and brothers to roll one of their prostrate forms out of her way, so that she could lug the ceramic water-jug up the steps. Sławek did not mind. His profits boomed, and he and his family just ate and ate, growing sleek and fat. Behind the house was Sławek's barn and distillery. He devoted a lot of time to the distillery, since it made him so much money. In winter, the cows lived in the barn with the pigs and the chickens. Brunek and Magda milked the cows each morning and evening. Maria attended to the needs of the pigs and the fowls.

MAGDA likes sleeping at the foot of her parents' bed. It is better to be sixteen, and respected, even if you have to do lots of work. She remembers what it was like when she shared the smaller room with the 'little kids', and six lay stacked each next to the other, their pee mixing together in a collective potato and pudding dream. That was before the three eldest were taken away: one by the army, one by the city, and one by marriage. The Germans have let the army one out of prison because he has a war wound, and he is married. He visits with his shy wife and three children once a week. The city one does not visit often. She works in Warsaw, in a real job, and earns real money. She is seeing a German soldier, and she worries about him, at the front. Her parents say she has no morals. She has a child, but no husband. She is welcomed anyway. She buys real presents for the children at Christmas: the delight on their faces makes up for the strange, fair, chiselled face of her child. Magda has never been to Warsaw. She would like to go. The married one lives in Małkinia, just over the horizon. She comes with her husband. She is pregnant, and seems to sail everywhere, the force of her size lending her grace, like the chiaroscuro ikon of the Virgin above the shop window.

Magda knows that she is next. Her father once barred her from seeing even the boy in the little shop that sold matches and cigarettes and cloth, but now he looks on approvingly, the sun reflecting off his bald pate, as she gazes at some of the Ukrainians dancing the Hopak in the street. Her face is heart-shaped, her glossy, black hair is parted into two long, thick braids. She rests her elbows on the sill, her chin lodged in her hands; she admires their movements, which are quick and liquid and skilful. Farmers and their children also watch, under the eye of the Virgin, the women clucking approvingly, drinking Juskowiak's vodka out of little earthenware tumblers. One of the Ukrainians, a lithe, muscular blond boy with a round, placid face, turns his flexible body over and over, hands to feet, windmilling through the air. Another claps time, singing, his voice clear and strong. The uniform jacket and the cap of the blond one hangs on a hook beside the Virgin. Magda can see the skull emblem on the cap. He dances in his black pants and braces; sweat runs down his back and chest. Her father says, 'You like one? The fair one?' He points, marking him out. He looks a strong boy. She has seen him before, shooting a Jew in the street. She liked his face then. She likes it now. Suddenly, he jabs the base of his palm on a small stone embedded in the earth. He leaps up, wringing his hand. 'Sorry, folks,' he puffs. 'Show's over.' He stumbles towards Magda, between two groups of applauding peasants, sweat streaking his tanned skin and gluing his hair to his head. He pulls a wad of banknotes out of his pocket, shoving them towards her. 'A bottle, please,' he grumbles. He belches, then belatedly covers his mouth. Magda sees that he has paid far too much money for one bottle, but she does not argue, complying with his demands.

'Who taught you to dance?'

'Father.'

'You are very good.' She speaks slowly, so he understands; his Polish is funny and halting. 'Your father must be a very clever man.'

'Was. He's dead. Jewish Bolsheviks killed him.' He leans against the wall, sucking directly from the bottle. He looks at her again. Now his eyes are bright and merry. She does not know who Jewish Bolsheviks are, only who the Jews are. Her father says they are bad people, who steal. Kazimier made a great mistake letting them come to Poland. He is still looking at her, although his eyes seem focused lower down, on her bodice. Her breasts would fit neatly in his large hands.

'What's your name?' he asks.

'Magda. What's yours?'

'Vitaly Fyodorovich.'

'Vitaly. That's a nice name.' She would like to smell his milky hair. She says, 'You're really fair.' He grunts comfortably, scratching the white hair on his chest.

'Born that way,' he admits. Maria and Sławek look at Vitaly. *He is strong. He will work hard.*

Magda smiles, turning to serve a newly arrived customer. Vitaly reaches through the window and lightly brushes her cheek with his fingertips. Her face reddens.

'Come on,' he says. 'Want to come for a walk?'

'In a minute.'

She looks at her father, who nods. He says, 'Not out of my sight.'

She steps out from behind the window and emerges through the front door, wiping her flour-dusted hands on her skirt. Vitaly hears the joyful cries of small children waft upwards and outwards as Maria serves them fried sausage and pickled cabbage at the big wooden table. Magda sits down on the step. He sits beside her, then leans forward and kisses her parted lips. 'Want some?' he asks, proffering the bottle. She smiles, touching the wet place on her mouth where he kissed her. He smells like vodka. 'All right.' She takes it from him. An old woman passes her one of the tumblers. *Shameless, kissing that Trawniki boy right in front of everyone like that.* Her father is watching them through the shutters, showing a wide, watery, toothless grin. The Virgin is smiling: her eyes are painted so that she looks directly at passers-by. The old women shake their heads, and remain silent. Maria's wrinkles reorient themselves into an expression matching her husband's. Magda takes a lock of Vitaly's frosted hair between her thumb and index finger, examining it closely. *That really is an amazing colour.* Vitaly's erstwhile dancing companions are sitting on the wooden flooring leading up to the shutters, hands draped around their knees, puffing.

'Ay, Vitaly, you want your jacket?'

'Naw. He won't need it. He's gonna take all his clothes off shortly and fuck that pretty girl.'

The Poles sitting on the decking do not understand their coarse, informal Ukrainian. Magda looks at the two of them. One, Karol, that's his name, has sly, wet-looking eyes that scare her. The other one, Johan, a big, sour-faced nineteen-year-old Volksdeutsche with curly, deformed eyebrows that meet in the middle licks his chops. He grins, a little tight grin. 'Women!' he hisses in Polish. 'Cunts!'

Shameless, on the step, Magda and the Trawniki boy are kissing. She is amazed at the flinty hardness of his boy's body. He sees that she has a scattering of amber freckles down her nose and across her cheeks.

'I'VE GOT a beautiful girl,' Vitaly brags that evening, in the barracks. Shura sits on his bunk, arms folded, listening. 'Which one?'

'Not a prostitute. A good girl. The girl in the vodka shop.'

'That one? The dark pretty one with the two long plaits and the big tits?'

'That one. I'm gonna get her a gold necklace, and a fur coat for the winter.'

Shura picks between his teeth with a twig and half closes his eyes, thinking.

'She's very pretty. I think the bull jumped the fence there. She's got brown eyes. Maria and Sławek both got blue. Where you going to fuck?'

'Barn behind her house, prob'ly. Lots of nice warm hay in there.'

Two days later, Magda began sleeping with Vitaly. A week later, he took her to Warsaw and booked a room at The White Eagle. They took their time. The hotel room was heated, so their lust was marked by a degree of languor not available at home in the barn. She liked this ease, this sloth. He said in response, 'You are the loveliest, sexiest girl I have ever met. Ever.'

EVEN BEFORE she began sleeping with Vitaly, Magda had learned about some of the Ukrainians. Karol Rohozin was the most fascinating. He had been a communist, in a Communist Party NKVD school, and had changed sides, betraying three hundred NKVD men to the Germans. The communists had deported his parents to Magadan and sent him to be educated in a 'proper' establishment. His parents were not anti-Stalin, but the boy had been born out of wedlock. Therefore, he was morally suspect. He spoke beautiful Polish, like a local, after only four months of sporadic visits to the town. He was lean and beaky, sort of like a crow, she thought. But she was scared of Rohozin, and some of the other Ukrainians. They marched into town, singing all the time. They sang 'Lili Marlene' with alternative lyrics. The lyrics were not nice. They were about having sex with dead women's bodies. They also sang the marching song of the Polish army, 'We, the First Brigade'. It had new coarse words as well. Kapepwi made up these words.

Johan Kapepwi, the Volksdeutsche, had been in the same NKVD school as Rohozin. His parents were also deported to Siberia. He was very clever, but when he asked the wrong questions of his teachers, the NKVD would suspend him upside down by his ankles overnight in the assembly hall. Just before the Germans reached Vinnitsa, where the school was located, he had calmly left a physics class, stating that he needed to use the toilet. He had gone to his locker, torn up his schoolbooks and used them as kindling to torch the school's political science wing. She could see him tearing his big thick Marxist textbooks down their spines weakened from use. He had told her how many volumes there were in *Das Kapital*. 'Lots. They burn well,' he told her. Then, as the corridor where the student's lockers were located was consumed in the conflagration, he had returned to his physics class, T-square in hand, and, before his stunned classmates, had cornered the teacher and beaten him to a bloody pulp. *Soon, we are going to have pickled Russian penis right in this building*. The Ukrainians in the class turned on the Russians and Jews, and, copying their new teacher, commenced beating them to similarly bloody pulps. Rohozin, his best friend, fresh from Marxism-Leninism II, was busy betraying the school's garrison to the Germans. The Germans put the NKVD in large pens underneath a red-brick building designated over its lintel 'Stalin Chemistry Building'. Kapepwi had slowly stalked upstairs, to one of the laboratories on the top floor of the chemistry block, and, dripping T-square still in hand, had pushed the window open and yelled to the captured NKVD beneath 'Are you ready to internalise some shit?' Then he had started to pour bottle after bottle of concentrated sulphuric acid down on the heads of his communist masters. The men stampeded, and their Wehrmacht guards opened fire. Corpses littered the asphalt.

She noticed that his Ukrainian was odd and halting, like his Polish. This was because he had been taught only Russian in the school: his own language had withered on his tongue.

Ivan M. had never been a communist, for he had never once lived in a communist country. He had played first division football for L'vóv, in the Polish football league, when there was no Ukraine and L'vóv was the de facto national team. She had seen him before on cigarette cards. He had a round, clean-cut face with bright, snapping grey eyes and shiny, healthy skin, ideally suited to cigarette cards. In the pictures, he had a mane of flowing black hair. The Germans made him keep it bristly short, prompting the usual 'Ivan-had-a-haircut-looks-like-a-coco-nut' taunts from his comrades. He had the SS runes excised into the short hair on the back of his head, about three inches high. Magda noticed them one day when he pulled his skull-emblem cap off before playing a game of mock serious football with some teenagers in the street. Crowds of children followed him around the town, and he chatted with them. He had mastered the clever showmanship associated with professional football, and the youngsters would stand in awe while he bounced a football from his head, to his chest, to his knees, to his feet and back to his head again. He remembered when the Piłsudski government had refused to allocate funds to schools in Polish West Ukraine. When it refused to lay sewerage pipes in L'vóv. The tattered textbooks and overworked teachers. The 'no-walk zone' beside every apartment block. 'Beware! Falling Shit!' The signs should have read. 'Don't go there,' rich Poles would tell their children. 'The Ukrainians don't go to the toilet properly. They pee out of the windows. It's a Ukrainian habit.' Ivan M. scared her also. If he wanted anything, he felt he should have it. He never visited the prostitutes who often came to the town. He said he didn't *need* that.

They stared at her, their eyes slippery with lust. They slept with prostitutes who came all the way from Warsaw, they made a lot of noise, and swore filthy words, even in Polish, which some of them did not know very well. They called Jews *kurwamac* and *kurwysyn*, which meant mother and son of menstrual blood. They even said this to each other. Sometimes she saw the trainloads of prisoners being sent towards the camp. The camp must have a lot of prisoners, she thought. The Germans had magic to make them disappear so suddenly and completely. If you walked up the hill, you could see its brush fence in the distance, topped at each corner by a wooden watchtower. Once she felt sure that she could see the sun glinting off Vitaly's white hair in one of the watchtowers. It seemed very large, large enough for many prisoners. Drunken guards treated the Jews very badly, deliberately frightening them by shooting into the air above the trains, or by opening the doors and firing at random into the packed flesh. She learnt to tell the difference between the sound of shot wood and the sound of shot flesh. The soft 'rrrip' of flesh. There was always blood on the railway tracks. She once saw Vitaly do this. She confronted him the next morning.

'You shot people in the trains last night. You woke every-body up, then kept doing it right in front of the whole town.'

'Did I?'

'Look at the mess there now. See. You did that.'

'I can't remember.'

'You should remember. I don't want you doing that at night. I want you in bed with me, like a proper husband.'

'But we are not. . .not married.'

'As good as.'

But one night she had been woken by thumping noises followed by a strange, mournful keening from near the front door. She had gone to investigate, sliding from beneath Vitaly's protective arm. She looked through the shutters. There she saw a Ukrainian, only fifteen or so, crying, sitting on the steps. He had an automatic rifle across his knees. His gangly, adolescent hand rested on the butt. He was hitting the back of his head repeatedly against the wooden bannister, slowly, deliberately, the action originating in his shoulders. He cried as he moved, his thin wail made irregular as he hit his head. Flakes of whitewash had settled on the collar of his summer uniform; she could see them in the moonlight. When he heard the shutters creak as she opened them, he looked at her, startled. 'What's the matter?' she whispered. He looked around him, furtively.

'I don't like what I. . .what happens. . .what we do—' He looked up; his dark brown eyes filled. 'I. . .we. . .do bad things, Pani. Bad things. . .and I'm scared. I'm scared all the time.'

In the morning there was blood on the bannister, and a fat, brown blotch on the slat flooring beneath, oddly symmetrical, like a Rorschach ink-blot. It could have been a spider or a bat. Or a flower.

She had seen the crying boy a few times since, and he had seemed just like the others, laughing and singing and dancing with electric skill. He did not scare her. Once he told her that the Germans said he could starve to death in the POW camp, or come to Treblinka as a guard. He came to Treblinka. He said it was terrible in the POW camp. The guards were Estonians. They could not tell the difference between Russians and Ukrainians, so they beat everybody. She noticed that he was very kind and gentle to his woman, and did not swear. He took the train to Małkinia every second Sunday so that he could attend Mass. He gave her father an ikon for the shopfront.

She was not afraid of Nikolai either, who had a normal plain wife in the town and three taffy-haired young children. Nikolai's only regret was that his children did not resemble him. His hair was black and glossy, his eyebrows beetling: his children seemed so fair that if cut, she fancied that they would bleed white. Just the sun on their fair eyelids made their eyelashes quiver; water beaded them like the moisture gathered on spider's webs on dewy mornings. But the Germans liked Nikolai's children. They said so, loud and often. They liked Vitaly also. She heard the tall German from Czechoslovakia say Vitaly was 'a fine Aryan specimen'. She asked Rohozin what 'specimen' meant, and he told her. Nikolai carved little wooden toys for his own children and the children of others; horses on wheeled bases and dolls with moving arms and legs. Stupid, harmless Voronikov helped him. Voronikov was actually a better carpenter than Nikolai, but he did not care to show it. He was happier with children. He spent hours devising games for the smallest child, and he joined in their play. Nowak swung from his hair. He gave Anna and Leokadja piggyback after piggyback. He played tiggy endlessly in the fields, his head bobbing up and down as he ran, his limbs hopelessly uncoordinated. 'He's got sand between his ears,' said Sławek looking at Voronikov's curly bowed head; 'Nothing but sand. But he's a wonder with children.' Nikolai did not like his work. He discussed it, frequently. He said he had to work with a madman, a man who was two eggs short of a dozen. Magda asked Vitaly about the madman. Vitaly said 'He's telling fibs. He only has to work there when Ivan T. has a rostered day off. He hardly ever has to work with Ivan T.' 'But is Ivan T. really mad?' she wanted to know. 'Oh, yes. The "T" is for "Terrible"; he means nothing by it, but he scares Nikolai. He is mad because the Jews burnt his house down in front of him. With his parents and six brothers and sisters inside. In the famine.'

She saw Ivan the Terrible the very next day, walking to catch the train to Małkinia. Vitaly said he had a girlfriend in Małkinia. He was very tall, with a calm, mild face and sandy hair; he was plainly of great strength. His expression was, she thought, thoroughly Ukrainian in its complete absence of curiosity or desire. Magda said 'He doesn't look mad.' Sławek leaned through the shutters, hawking his wares. 'Vodka, poppy-seed cake, sausage, Pan Ivan. Some flowers for Panna

Romana?' Ivan walked over to the shop in a leisurely fashion, hands hanging loosely at his sides. He spoke so softly that Sławek had difficulty understanding his order, and he waited patiently while Magda fetched and carried, singing to himself. He had a startlingly clear and thrilling voice. Magda asked 'What song do you sing, Pan Ivan?' he smiled at her, the skin around his eyes and mouth crinkling from finding many things funny. 'Oh, I make it up as I go along.' He turned away slowly, still humming. 'He is not mad,' she said to Vitaly. Vitaly laughed, his merry, deep 'you don't know what you're on about' laugh. 'Ivan has passion', he said. It was true. Once, on one of his regular trips to the Juskowiak's for 'provisions', she chanced to look into his eyes. They were the colour of slate; dead, without joy. The smile lines had fooled her at first, but his humour was all hate.

This information aside, it must be said that Magda loved Vitaly, especially his lopsided grin. She felt content in his presence, and would do everything she could to make him produce that grin, which he did, often. 'Look at your hair!' he would gasp, slowly unbraiding it prior to lovemaking. 'It comes down past your cunt!' He kneaded her breasts, and whispered swear words into her hair. His own hair fell in a boyish, haphazard way over his forehead, clashing in an attractive way with the skull and crossbones on his field cap. His mouth was full and moist, with a small pink 'v' in the cleft of his lower lip. His tongue caressed it, then darted out as he moved close enough to lick the whorl of her ear. She curled her small body inside the semicircle of his large body, and was tickled by the soft hair on his chest.

His lusts were simple and defined, and, at least partly due to the practices he had enjoyed in Warsaw, reasonably skilled. Maria heard them making love in the barn with real earnestness, and noted how her daughter always returned flushed and merry after her periodic trips to Warsaw with Vitaly.

Thus, she counted out some prayers for her poor wayward daughter, who was surely fornicating herself to damnation.

Magda also noticed, when she slept with him, that his back was covered with terrible white scars. The scars stood out: she could feel them through his shirt. She asked him why. The Jewish and Russian Bolsheviks beat him, he said. Tied him up to a post and flogged him. There was no reason.

Sometimes he came home from work smelling bad, and he said that no matter how much he washed, he could never get the smell of kerosene and cooked meat out of his hair. He brought her nice clothes. Occasionally he got drunk and smashed things, and once when he broke three of Maria's pottery dinner plates in an especially wild night of drunken abandon, he promised to make good double the number. Maria had been sceptical. 'He may be good for clothes,' she said, 'but crockery is not something you just call up out of the earth.' The next day he appeared with a cardboard box stacked with an entire dinner set, made of improbably fine china, creamy white, decorated with small blue flowers. Sławek, who could read a little, said that the letters impressed on the back of each piece were in the Latin alphabet, like Polish words, and said 'Wedgwood'. The dinner set pleased Maria, who forgave him, and kissed him on the forehead as a gesture of respect.

Vitaly worked hard on the Juskowiak farm when he could, enlisting the aid of a few other Ukrainians to build another room for the house. He also supplied Magda with a fur coat, a gold friendship ring, a necklace and a silk negligee. She considered the latter amusing. So did he. He helped with the potato harvest, and was strong and hardy, doing the work of a draughthorse in the fields. Because of this, when they slept together, first in the barn, and later in the room Vitaly had built, Sławek and Maria said nothing, apart from Maria's fitful prayers. Magda was not married, but she clearly had a husband. Feelings in the town followed similar paths. If old

Juskowiak had acquired a strong, hardworking Ukrainian to help with the farm work and the potato harvest, the villagers reasoned, then good luck to him. To the curious, who might wonder how Sławek paid the Ukrainian, or why he would want to work such a poor holding, there was Magda, whose broad hips and strong legs bespoke of the harvest that might be reaped between them by such a lusty young man. Other women also formed liaisons with Askaris; they would wait beside the rail terminus for their men each week. Off-duty times were rotated fortnightly, and so a different clump of women would appear on alternate Fridays. Sometimes Polish children would cluster around their older sisters. When the camp was first being built, and the Askaris had first came to the locality, these children would chant in unison at the uncomprehending Ukrainians, 'Headhunter Headhunter Headhunter Askar'. Vitaly remembered the chanting vividly: groups of pink-cheeked Polish children yelling sing-song loud and flat, apparently for his benefit. When Magda told him what it meant, he laughed. 'Why do they say that? Do they see the Jews coming through?'

'Everyone sees the trains coming through. It's because you're not,' she groped for the long and complex word that she had heard Rohozin use, '*not civilised*. The children see the Jews hanging out of the windows in the trains, all dirty and starved, and put you people together with that. Not, *civilised*. You know.' Sometimes the Polish children would yell at the Jews, also. 'Jews, you're going to be made into fertiliser' or 'Jews, they're turning you into soap.' She had told him about the crying boy and the blood on the step. Yes, he'd seen the patch of blood. No, he did not know why, but the Germans were bastards, they might have made him do something awful. 'What do you mean by "awful?"' she asked, but he could not elaborate.

It was an issue of great magnitude: *civilisation*. Why she was civilised and he was not. The Polish children who had yelled 'Headhunter Headhunter Headhunter Askar' at the railway station smiled at him when he walked past them with his arm around Magda's waist, his black uniform pressed and smart. Her civilised presence seemed to reassure them that there were no rings of small, dried ears around his neck, no bones through his nose. This civilisation had an order to it: it sang Christmas carols (which he liked, and was good at), it promenaded in summer and autumn, so that he could give the children sweets, it went to the pictures in Warsaw, then found a quiet place in the Saxon Gardens to kiss and cuddle. Poles would walk past, pretending not to look, but looking anyway. Often they thought the fair man was a German, but if they walked by close enough they saw the blue and yellow flag stitched to the sleeve of his uniform, and knew that he was not. Once a man from the *Armia Krajowa* stopped behind them, watching the German soldier gently twine the Polish girl's hair in his fingers. Impotent anger rose in him. The Germans were buying the women of his country. The soldier looked up, and, in heavily accented speech, wished him a good evening. The Pole saw the flag on his uniform, looked at the young woman with her arms draped around his neck, and wished them a pleasant night as he walked away. *How do you deal with cases like that?*

When Vitaly and Magda fucked together, noisily, he felt he might imbibe some of her civilisation, the way he recklessly imbibed vodka after a shift. But her subdued habits vanished in bed. 'He's a good farmer and loyal, you work at keeping him,' Maria ordered, her piety forgotten. She grabbed his hair, pulling it, and his back was covered with more white marks from her cats-claw scratches. His appetites ran to impromptu sex against walls or deep within warm haystacks. Her hands would corkscrew into his clothes, her fingers finding what they wanted with unerring and surprising accuracy.

In her dreams, she wanted him to adopt the part of hardworking farmer, and would watch him walking through the fields, out of uniform, clad in a loose shirt and pants gathered at the ankles, scythe carried across his shoulders. Her father approved of him also. 'He works hard,' he said. 'He loves you and does not look at other women. He is handsome—I know you like his face—and not clever enough to want to run away. He is also pious. Each night he lights a candle before his ikon, and says prayers. I've stood and watched him.' She knew something of the nature of his work, because once he had come to her with blood on his uniform, and this scared her. When the wind blew from the camp across the village, she could hear the dull racket of machinery stopping and starting, rifle shots, and the pungent smell of burnt meat. But she did not ask. He would have told her had she done so. Other women asked their Askari husbands what they did for a living, and were told.

MAGDA: 'I did love him, even though he sometimes annoyed me. Sometimes I couldn't stand to be next to his stinking drunk self. But most of the time, he was considerate and sweet, and very hardworking. He was such a strong man, and would work all day on his day off to get something done for my father. He took me to the movies in Warsaw, and brought me nice clothes, things I never had before. He also loved me good in bed. I remember the first time we did it, we couldn't wait to get our clothes off and were half undressed before we got to the barn. Then we made so much noise that we woke up Mama's chickens and started the rooster crowing. She thought a fox was loose in the barn, and came across the yard to look. He always said he wanted to find my 'magic spot'. It was like being tickled all over, but good tickled. Father Wajda of Małkinia, when he came to our village, told some of the women with Askari men that it was bad to like it so much, that only loose women liked it like that. I think they felt bad for about one day, then everything went back to normal. They gave that priest nothing but a hard time.

He was also very happy when I told him I was pregnant. I know that you can't say all people are the same as each other, but I think all Ukrainians love children, they love lots of children, and are very kind fathers. Vitaly did a backflip right in the street when I told him. It was lovely how he got me all sorts of nice things when I was pregnant. I liked being pregnant. When I started to get big, Vitaly and I would talk to it, and tell it all about the family, and things. He would tap out a tune on my tummy with his fingers, and sing. My parents thought Vitaly was very sweet to me, especially since they felt I gave him too much lip for a good wife.

Vitaly also made it good on festival days. Always, the Podlassia part of Poland has been poor, but the Ukrainians made us rich. Vitaly brought me things, and Papa had baskets of jewellery that the Ukrainians used to pay their bills with when they ran out of money. Vitaly and Voronikov would bring chocolate and plum schnapps and slivovitz and lots of cured ham down to our house and the village would get together with the Ukrainians and have a really good time. People would look at Shura and Mohammed Yerlan Tian and the other Kazakhs—there were four of them—and wonder how they came to be that funny colour, all brassy yellow. They did not mind having lots of attention. They laughed. Even Ivan called 'the Terrible' seemed happy, drinking and telling dirty jokes, although he had a basilisk's stare, which we carefully avoided. My mother would fry the ham until all the lard had been rendered and we would eat bread and ham and soft cheese and plums until we all thought we were going to burst. Father and my brothers-in-law would get very drunk, sometimes throwing up in the yard so that they could come back and drink more. In the summer, people finished up scattered all over the house by the next morning, or would have sex in the barn while other people watched. When Ivan the Terrible got really drunk, sometimes he produced a gramophone and played jazz and swing records for people to dance to out in the yard. He sat beside it, clapping his hands on his knees in time to the music. He had very good timing, and enjoyed his little concerts. How the drink flowed! My Father stayed in bed for a whole two days after the Christmas we had in 1942.'

OFTEN SHE waited for him beside the railway terminus, and he would reach out as far as he could and take her hand. She smiled at him, always in the same way, her short nose wrinkling appealingly. He traced the line of her eyebrow with his finger, saying, 'At least you've got an eyebrow. It's more than I've got.' Sometimes, in summer, she would sleep in the afternoons, and he would creep into their room after work, trying not to disturb her. He knew that she could hear him, and that she only pretended to be fast asleep, but he did not like to be loud. He would stoop over the bed, smooth back her hair and kiss her mouth. He would say, softly, 'you fancy a good screw now, or you want to wait for a bit?' She would roll towards him, open one eye, and say 'now' or 'later', depending on her preference.

'She's a good woman,' he told Shura. 'Never looks anywhere else. Loves only me.' It was true. She did love only him. The good woman.

VITALY and Magda took little Anna to the movies in Warsaw, to see an American movie called *Fantasia*. Voronikov and Shura had seen it, and had recommended it highly. They said it had monsters in it, but not truly scary monsters, except at the end. The German authorities did not like to show American movies, now that America was 'The Enemy', but there was nothing better to show in Warsaw, so Governor Frank had given his permission. He said that his dispute was with Mr Roosevelt, not with Mr Disney. Voronikov also said the movie was in colour, with lots of nice music. There were some English words, but not enough to spoil the movie.

Anna had never even left Treblinka before, and she pressed her nose up against the windows of the train, watching the towns and farms go by, while Vitaly and Magda chatted. She bounced up and down. 'Look! Look!' she shouted when the train stopped in the bustling Małkinia station, its platform crowded with soldiers and civilians. Some of the civilians were waving. A big German private kept people back from the track. He shook his rifle in the air. A dead body lay beside the private's feet, its head resting in a pool of blood. Two Polish police officers were putting chalk marks around it. Magda gasped. 'A murder! Someone's been murdered! How terrible!' Vitaly stared dumbly at the activities on the platform, chewing his lip. Sweat prickled on his back. Anna clambered over Vitaly's lap, straining to see more from the train window. Vitaly winced as she trod on his groin. 'Come on, Anna,' he growled, 'behave. Do you want to pee?' She nodded. Vitaly took her hand, leading her towards the toilet. He sighed. Magda looked up at him, giggling fiendishly. 'You'll have to get used to it. You know that I'm six months now. You'll have your own, soon.' He bent down, putting his ear on her rounded belly. Her heavy dirndl almost hid the roundness. 'Can you feel it?' she asked.

'Ooo, yes. I think he'll be a footballer, the way he kicks.'

Anna tugged at his arm. 'Come *on!*'

Anna spent large parts of the movie in Vitaly's lap, then, during the dinosaur sequence, insisted on sitting between them. She buried her head in Vitaly's duffle coat during 'Night on Bald Mountain', but laughed at the dancing hippos and elephants. She clapped her hands in glee for the centaurs and satyrs, and Vitaly watched as her face was lit with bright splashes of colour. He wondered what the strange monsters

THE HAND THAT SIGNED THE PAPER

were, and wished fervently that he could read the Polish subtitles. Vitaly felt sure that Anna had annoyed the old Polish couple who sat directly behind them enough to warrant a complaint to the usher. 'Shh,' he kept hissing. 'You're wriggling too much.' He heard the old Polish woman chuckle. He swung around sharply. The two Poles stared at him, fear realigning their features. 'I'm so sorry,' he whispered. 'She's never come to Warsaw before, never seen a movie, not even a no colour one.' The old woman allowed herself to smile. She beamed at Anna. 'Behave for your Daddy. There's a good girl.' Anna cocked her tawny head on one side, producing her cutest expression. 'He's not my Daddy. He's my brother-in-law.' The old man tousled her hair, fondly.

After the film, Vitaly produced a large block of chocolate in the foyer and gave it to the Polish couple, apologising profusely as he did so. 'Thank you for not complain about us. . .I hope she not spoil the film.'

'*Mein Herr*, thank you for so much chocolate; we will save it for our grandchildren, but we would never complain about you.' The old man leaned close to Vitaly's chest, whispering. 'It is not permitted to complain about any SS men, even Slavic ones. You are not Polish; where are you from?'

'From Ukraine, from Khmel'nik. But my Polish is getting better.'

Anna took the hand of the old woman. 'You've got a nice face,' she said, smiling. 'For someone who is so old. You must be the oldest person in Poland.'

IT IS TRUE, the people in the country age quickly, there are few old folks there. Anna once had thirteen brothers and sisters, now there are only eight. The old couple are not insulted. The man in his German uniform is smartly attired, but the woman and the child are dressed in the heavy home-sewn clothes of peasants, people who do not often travel over the horizon or past the line of trees. The woman is very young, and already pregnant. The monied Ukrainian beside her simply allows her to enjoy her brief bloom more fully. The old man thanks Vitaly for the chocolate once again—even in the city, this is a rare item—then turns away, dignified and upright. Anna takes Magda's hand, and resumes her previous activity of admiring the city, particularly its wonderful electric light. Vitaly hooks his long arm around Magda's waist.

WHEN SHE was visiting Warsaw with Vitaly, Magda saw a round-up. '*Achtung Judenaktion. Alle Juden heraus.*' She watched as a very few Germans and Ukrainians stood on the footpath, while Jewish militiamen used staves to beat their own people with an energy she had not thought possible. Some of the Jewish children were already dead, their heads crushed by the heavy timber. Magda covered her mouth, feeling bile rise in her throat. Finally, one of the Ukrainians pulled the most active of the Jewish militiamen away from his quarry, and waved his rifle in the air. She could hear him yelling, but not what he said. 'How, Vitaly, how do they? Is it because the kapos were poor, and the others rich?'

Vitaly said, 'In my village, the kommissar was Ukrainian. He always sat before a loaded plate while we starved. We could see him through the window. It is like that.'

HALF-A-DOZEN prostitutes from Warsaw moved into the vacant flat above the butcher shop. Tadek, the butcher, did not complain, because they paid their rent promptly each fortnight. Sometimes, he would be startled by the strange noises emanating from above, and the clunk of booted feet on the steps at the rear sometimes woke his wife and three small children, but he was left alone. People chuckled at Tadek the Butcher. Hot meat upstairs, they said, and cold meat down.

The prostitutes themselves were not suffering stereotypes, their innocence destroyed by some rape or long-lost love, but shrewd women who made money from generous peasants like the Ukrainians because it was easy. In all probability they hated the men who came to them, men with blood still matted in their short, wavy hair. Some of them, like Voronikov, cried out for their dead mothers at the peak of their love heat, or would be reduced to babbling incoherence by vodka and memory. The prostitutes took the bloody złoty, paid Tadek their rent and bought an ikon from the markets in Małkinia. It was displayed over their back door, at the top of the steps, beside the toilet. Anna would visit Tadek and the prostitutes, and run small errands for them, for which she would be paid a few groszy. The prostitutes had lots of pretty clothes, but her mother said they were indecent. Most of the villagers thought their painted faces strange. They sat out on the small landing above the butchery in the summer and autumn, talking quietly among themselves, drinking vodka that the Ukrainians brought to them from the camp and from her father's. She walked past them on her way to Tinka's. Tinka's father was a richer farmer than Anna's, because, as Maria said, he had only five children, and because his wife was a Volksdeutsche, and thus was paid an allowance by the Germans. Anna stopped before Tadek's, and looked up towards the landing. Two of the prostitutes were seated on it, on wooden stools. 'Hello Pani Viktoria, Hello Pani Lena,' she called.

Viktoria looked over the balcony. 'Anna! Where you going?'

'Tinka's place.'

'Come in and eat some pie. You're as skinny as a mongrel dog.'

'Mama says I can't.'

Viktoria had pretty purple all around her eyes. She did all the talking. Lena never talked. She just sang, soft and low, not in Polish. She was fatter than Viktoria, and her hair was always in paper curlers. Viktoria said the songs were in Latvian, Lena came from Latvia. Anna didn't know where Latvia was. And Viktoria also said they were religious songs. Lena was singing now.

'Pani Viktoria, what's she singing? Is it Latvian?'

'Lord in Heaven, I don't know. It's English, I think, you know, British.'

Lena shook her head. 'American,' she said. It was the only spoken word Anna ever heard pass through Lena's lips. Lena started to sing, pure and clear, louder than before, her voice making farmer Milewski in his cart look up from his reins as his horse ambled up the street.

'Mine Eyes have seen the glory of the comin' of the Lord, He is stampin' out the vintage where the grapes of wrath is stored. . .

'I saw an American movie. It was called *Fantasia*.'

'Was it good?'

'Ooo, yes. It had dancing elephants in it. And crocodiles.'

Viktoria rolled her eyes. 'Americans!' She said, emphatically. 'You still haven't answered my question. You going to come in and have some pie?'

'Mama says I can't'

'Why?'

'She says you're an indecent woman.'

Pani Viktoria laughed, raising her skinny arms to the sky. '*What* a town!' she muttered. 'What a *town.*'

Later that evening, when Anna was in bed, her little brother's arm sticking into her side, she heard the Ukrainians spending the night with Pani Viktoria and Pani Lena and their sisters singing the American song. They sang it over and over, they liked it so much. 'He has loosed the fatal lightnin' of his terrible swift sword, His truth is marchin' on! Glory, Glory, Alleluia, Glory, Glory. . .' Then they started on the song that she knew was their National Song, because Vitaly had told her it was. It was very beautiful, but terribly sad. '*Shche ne vmerla Ukrayina, Shche ne. . .*'

Once, an engineer from Warsaw, Jerzy, had visited Tadek early one morning to buy some salted pork cutlets to cook for his lunch. Anna saw him walk into the shop. His firm was doing some building in the district, he later explained. Jerzy waited underneath a row of cool carcasses as Tadek served a heavily built Ukrainian SS man, accepting the offer of two men's wristwatches in exchange for a leg of mutton. Jerzy leaned forward when he saw such an unequal exchange. 'Where did you get those watches?' He picked one up. 'That's a Rolex. It would be worth nearly four-hundred złoty.' The grin on Tadek's face widened. He pointed at the Ukrainian.

'Ask him. He works there.' Tadek turned to his watch-paying customer. 'Ay, Voronikov. The man wants to buy a watch from you.' Jerzy tried to shake his head and back away, but Voronikov had already produced another dozen watches from the pockets of his uniform. He displayed them on the counter, disentangling them with podgy fingers.

'For this one, for a Pani, twenty złoty. This for Pan,' he indicated to Jerzy. 'Only ten złoty. Best quality.'

Jerzy swallowed. 'Where did you get them so cheaply— those are good watches.'

'From Treblinka.'

'But this is Treblinka.'

'From camp. Up that way. I am on staff there.'

'Did you take them from the Jews?'

'Only dead Jews.'

'You kill Jews?'

Voronikov bent his head forward, rolling his eyes and clutching at his throat, making small, strangled noises. Tadek started to laugh, a deep, gurgling sound that originated in his sternum. Voronikov, behind his grunts and wheezes, was also laughing. Jerzy stepped backwards, towards the door, slamming into one of the prostitutes. 'Look out where you're going, will ya!' she yelled. She wriggled past him. She was dressed in an ankle-length sable coat and leather court shoes. Jerzy watched as she stared at Voronikov's imitation of strangulation, her lip raised in a sneer. Her face, without the sneer, was quite pretty; but she was wearing too much purple make-up. She saw the watches on the counter and smiled. Voronikov stood upright, still chuckling. She sidled up to him, rubbing her hand up his chest. 'Hey, big boy. I give you a good time for just one of those. Real good time.' He let her unbutton his fly, and his face became slack-jawed. Saliva ran down his chin. Jerzy clutched himself with folded arms, trying to dispel a sudden chill. He closed his eyes. Suddenly, Tadek clapped his hands. 'Aie. Not that in my shop. Upstairs or in town, but not in my shop.' Voronikov nodded in agreement, licking his lips and cradling her face in his blunt, calloused fingers. 'I gotto take this meat to Vitaly and Magda. I promised them. You want to come for walk? Then we come back and fuck?'

JERZY the well-educated engineer from Warsaw sees in Voronikov's face the definition of Lavater's 'Criminal Type'. He has already observed the new buildings on the farms and the women in their fine furs, only a month before Christmas, but now he has seen everything. The coarse, handsome face with its low, curly hairline and glittering emerald irises glares at him every time he shuts his eyes. He must work in this district for some time, he knows that. Each morning he will see these people. When he catches the train to Siedlce he passes the establishment that feeds the town its watches, gold and inflated currency, that pays for its expensive Warsaw tarts. He saw it this morning, or the brush that concealed it, at least. He saw some of its inmates, gathering brush outside the gates, guarded by tall Ukrainians with cocked rifles and a short German with a whip. People on the train had flocked to the window to look, pointing and chattering. Both the prisoners and their guards saw the passengers staring. One of the Ukrainians waved. The prisoners simply stared. The German had his back turned. Jerzy does not yet know what Voronikov's eye-rolling demonstration of asphyxiation means, and for a month or so, it seems that the town is conspiring to conceal its guilty secret from him. If he walks past a cluster of Poles or Ukrainians talking among themselves, the silence produced is immediate and embarrassing in its intensity. Occasionally, Jerzy sees German staff cars roar through the town, spinning their wheels in the icy dirt, spraying mud over the legs of innocent bystanders. *It is just a little town with a population of 150* he thinks, like every other little town around this German establishment. Eventually, he hears of what they have done to the village. This village. One Polish girl tells him, 'Such a lovely name, and such a beautiful village, considering what they do here.'

ANNA liked Christmas, not just because of the presents, but because of the relatives and friends from other villages. She saw her father deep in drunken discussion with her big brother Władisław, who limped now from his war wound. Władisław was funny. Vitaly and her big sister Magda had been hard at it when he and his wife Tania arrived the day before, their cries and grunts sounding through the house. 'Stop tickling me, Magda!' Anna heard Vitaly yell. Pause. 'Don't start again! Awww!' 'Typical Ukrainian,' Władisław had said, loudly, reinforcing a local stereotype. 'If he's not screwing, he's drinking, and if he's not drinking, he's sleeping the drink off.' Vitaly and Magda had appeared shortly after, hair dishevelled, looking sheepish. Vitaly and Władisław struck up a conversation at once, and Magda looked at her brother with mean eyes. She did not think Władisław and Vitaly would like each other. But Władisław did not care that his sister lived with and obviously enjoyed a man dressed in a German uniform. He fought for Poland because of the call-up, and because they paid him. If he had been fit, and the Germans had required his services, he would have gone wherever they sent him, grumbling and whining, it is true. He complained, but if there was war, he went. He said he was past worrying, although his leg went completely stiff before wet weather. Very good forecaster, he said.

When Vitaly gave him a whole bottle of slivovitz to himself he retired to the corner, bottle in hand. He had consumed half the bottle when he decided to show everyone how well he could dance the mazurka. He spun around and landed on his backside, laughing. The Christmas celebration was the best he had ever seen, he told Anna. She laughed as Nikolai organised egg and spoon races for the hordes of children, and then gave out chocolate to anyone who joined in. She saw Voronikov stretch out on his stomach on the floor, eye to eye with little Nowak, his fingers twirling a multi-coloured spinning top, a Christmas gift. Nowak squealed with delight, a big bubble of warmth coming up from the pit of his stomach. Anna watched as well, giggling. Voronikov put his hand on her head, and smoothed back her hair, a movement telling in its gentleness. Later, Voronikov let off some rockets and firecrackers in the middle of the street. The children's faces were pale and awed by this blaze of speckled light. Tinka thought that angels had come to visit the village, leaving trails of angel dust behind them. Ivan the Terrible was having a private jazz concert beside the gramophone, wishing, no doubt, that he was Duke Ellington. He looked up from his imaginary piano and smiled at her. Even his eyes seemed to smile. 'Merry Christmas, Pan Ivan,' she said, 'and God bless you.'

'I hope Ivan M's having a good time,' he hissed. 'Rostered on on Christmas Eve. Poor shit.'

But after the presents had been distributed, and the food and drink mostly consumed, Anna was bored. Tinka sat in front of the fire, warming her outstretched hands. Maria was curved behind her, head resting on her arm, an empty vodka bottle in front of her face, which was smooth and unworried from drink. She snored. Her breath misted the slate. Several couples had retired to the barn to pursue their interests further, and Anna heard her father yell, 'Anyone touches that distillery and I'll bust their fucking face.' She saw Ivan the Terrible and Romana Sobeska from Małkinia talking earnestly in a corner of the kitchen. Ivan had his large hands on Romana's hips. Romana kept stroking Ivan's head, which bristled with a fresh crew cut. He hoisted her skirts above her waist, then lifted her gently onto the table. 'We'd better not watch,' said Tinka. 'We'd better look the other way.' Tinka pulled the grey curtain across the gap in the partition, and walked towards the back of the room. She looked outside. It was snowing steadily. Władisław was throwing up in the yard.

'What we going to do?' she asked.

'Dunno,' said Tinka.

'Go to bed, maybe.'

'Not tired.'

'We could look at Vitaly's dirty magazines.'

'Dirty magazines? Where?'

'He keeps 'em under his bed. Lots.'

Anna dragged some of the magazines from under the wooden double bed that Vitaly had built for Magda. One of them had a pretty, naked woman on the front, hanging from a hook in the ceiling, her wrists bound with chains. Inside was a photo of a woman sucking a man's huge, erect penis, her eyes looking indolently towards the viewer. There were oily fingerprints on the pages. Tinka gasped and covered her mouth. 'Does Magda know? About these?'

'They sit and look at them together. I've seen them.'

'Men use them to have sex with when they've got no wife,' Tinka said, knowingly. Her finger underscored the words on the front page, jerkily. 'It's German, they're German books. But I can't read it. It's too hard. My mother would be able to read it, but she says they're sinful.'

'But Vitaly don't need no dirty pictures. Him and Magda are always doing it. Once they did it four times in the one day. I counted.'

'How do you know?'

'They get all touchy with each other, kissing in the kitchen and things. They play footsie under the table, and Vitaly starts looking down Magda's dress. Then they come in here and do it. We can hear. And Magda's hair gets all mussed up.'

'Doesn't he work most of the time?'

'Yep. That's why they do it lots when he's not working. Even now Magda's getting big.'

Tinka's fine, new moon eyebrows arched. 'How?'

'She sits on top, like she's riding a horse.' Anna demonstrated, using her fingers. 'I even heard her telling Vitaly to giddy-up horse, once.'

Vitaly stumbled into the bedroom, dragging Magda behind him. She kept tripping over her own feet, giggling, and saying, 'I'm too drunk, sugar plum, I'll fall asleep.' Both drunken eagerness and embarrassment were apparent on Vitaly's face, especially when he saw the children. Anna hastily shoved the magazines under the bed, and when one refused to go, she sat on it. Tinka presented her widest, sweetest smile. 'Good afternoon, Panie,' she said, then stood and curtsied before the swaying couple. Magda clutched her huge stomach. She belched, loudly. 'I shouldn't have had all that plum schnapps; I think I'm going to spew. . .' Anna finally succeeded in pushing the magazine under the bed and moved rapidly to one side as Magda vomited on the spot where she had sat. Vitaly adroitly kicked the chamber-pot under the flow, and only a little landed on the floor. He looked hard at Anna, suddenly sober. 'Water. Quick,' he said. 'Now!' Anna said,

'There's water on the stove.' Tinka said, 'But Ivan and Romana are there.'

The two girls edged around the kitchen table, avoiding Ivan's outstretched leg. He was on his back, head thrown to one side, with Romana curled on top of him. His giant frame covered most of the table-top. Most of their clothing was scattered on the floor, but Ivan had managed to drape his greatcoat across Romana's back. She was asleep, with one hand hooked around his head, the other resting on his chest. The tip of her thumb rested just inside the pink rim of her lips. His eyes were closed, and his face was very serene, but he was not asleep. He stroked her buttocks gently with one hand.

When Anna and Tinka returned, Vitaly had cleaned up the mess, and he and Magda sat on the edge of the bed, his arm around her shoulders. He spoke softly to her. Vitaly took the bucket and wooden ladle from Anna, and began wiping Magda's face with a damp cloth. Magda drank gratefully. Vitaly looked at Anna, then at Tinka. 'Magda's good girl. My fault she did this. My fault. Now you go to bed.'

MAGDA: 'When I come to having my baby, Vitaly wanted to take me to a proper hospital in Małkinia. He was very worried after I got sick from drinking so much on Christmas Eve, but that was only a one-off—I was good up until then and good after. He was a great one for dragging in doctors where we thought they wasn't needed, although now I know he was right. He got one of the Jew doctors from the concentration camp to give everyone smallpox shots, and something else as well—tetanus, I think. This poor Jew doctor looked so scared, although he wasn't starved. He had a big yellow stripe painted across his shirt, to show he was a Jew, although he had such a big nose he didn't need the stripe. I wouldn't go to hospital to have my baby, because the midwife, Ania, she knew more about babies than any doctor. But Vitaly got angry about this, and paid a doctor to come from Malkinia. The doctor was a Volksdeutsche, and you could tell he thought all Poles were grubby little disease-carriers. I suppose Vitaly paid him a lot of money, to make him come. I think Vitaly argued with the doctor, but I don't know. The doctor made Ania boil all my sheets, then lay them crisp and dry on the bed, and had Papa limewash the whole room from top to bottom, even the ceiling. He tried to boss Ania about, and made out that she didn't know anything. 'She's not even a registered nurse,' he said to Vitaly. But Vitaly stuck up for Ania. He said to just give me things to stop me hurting, and not interfere any more. 'Magda knows the midwife. You're a stranger.' he said.

VITALY sits outside with Sławek, Brunek and Piotr. The house is off-limits to men. They hear Magda howling and Sławek says, 'a lot of use that doctor was.' Vitaly chews his lip and keeps his arms folded, praying softly. He watches Sławek's fingers feed the rosary forward bead by bead, sees his lips moving slightly. He stands up. 'I must leave. My shift start soon.' Sławek looks up at him. 'Fuck them for German bastards,' he says. Vitaly closes his eyes before he walks away. Magda keeps crying; each scream seems to tear her apart. Vitaly crosses himself carefully. *'Ave Maria, Ave Maria. . .'*

When Vitaly returns nine hours later, breathless from sprinting, he sees Sławek dancing on the spot. Ania is seeing the doctor off. Sławek skips around them. The doctor turns and sees Vitaly. 'Congratulations! You have a beautiful son. Your eyes and your wife's hair. God bless!' Sławek waves now. The children are arranged outside, yelling. 'Come on Askar, raz-dwa, raz-dwa, you've got a son.' He draws up beside the door; Ania leads him inside. 'We cleaned up the mess,' she says. Magda is propped up on pillows and arranged on clean sheets. The baby is asleep on her chest. 'Look Vitaly. Isn't he lovely? What shall we call him? It was such hard work, and he's so little. So tiny. I thought babies were bigger.' The women laugh. *So many things you don't know, but what do you expect? She is a child; he means well, but is none too bright.* Vitaly takes her face in his hands. 'Do you like Ihor?' he asks, 'Ihor is a nice boy's name.' He kneels, strokes the child's downy head, kisses Magda. *'Non nobis, Domine, non nobis, sed nomini tuo da gloriam.'*

THE PRIEST drew his wet hand across Ihor's ruddy face. The child screamed. 'I bet that water's cold,' Sławek whispered. 'Ihor Bronisław Vitalyevich Kovalenko, do you renounce the Devil and all his works and all his ways?'

Outside the church. Photographs. Formal clothes. Admiring female relatives. Sweating children: a hot day, the first of an early summer. A hush echoed over the assembled. 'The priest! The priest! The father is coming!' The Father, a small grey man with clean hands, came down the front steps towards Vitaly and Magda. He stopped before them.

'It has passed to me that you have come into prosperous times.'

'Yes, Father,' Magda answered.

'Your son has a great name of the Church. After a saint.'

'A saint?'

'Yes. You can read of it in the holy works of the church.'

Vitaly looked at Ihor's downy head and thought *you will know what I can never know. You will go to school.*

The priest looked at Vitaly's pale blond hair, and his smartly pressed uniform.

'You have not come to the church.'

Magda stared intently at the priest's dark eyes. 'Now we have money, we will get married. Vitaly wishes it.'

'It is good that you think pure thoughts.'

The priest took Vitaly by the elbow, and led him into a

patch of shade by the vestry. He mopped his brow. 'It is terrible, this heat, and so early in the year.'

Vitaly nodded. 'Yes Father, it is terrible.'

'I hear, Herr Kovalenko, that you can get things. Clothes and books, and toys, from your work.'

'That is true.'

The priest squirmed in his vestments, ran a finger around the inside of his collar. *If only this Ukrainian would talk, and not stare so insolently at me!*

'We. . .ah. . .have an orphanage here in the Małkinia parish, to care for abandoned and unwanted children, and children whose parents have died. . .in the war, and so on. Poor things, they have no nice toys to play with, and their clothes are more patches than anything else.'

'Father, if you want clothes and toys for your orphanage, then I will get them. It is not hard, although I cannot be fussy, as the Germans do not like us to take things.'

'No, no. Of course not. Whatever you can get. We would be grateful. And. . .you will receive absolution. Your sins will be forgiven. . .if you can perform this small work for the church.' The priest sweated nervously. The Bishop was right. This Ukrainian was generous like the Ukrainians in Warsaw. Yet the Bishop was also wrong. Although this Ukrainian had an insolent cast of face, he was not a raving lunatic like the Bishop said the Warsaw Ukrainians were. It had been easy, really.

'I will get others to help you, if you like.'

The priest jerked his head up. 'Would they?'

'Oh, yes. They would get you as many things as you wanted for the orphanage. But the things must be boiled. There has been typhus in the camp.'

'Typhus? Why?'

'Because Jews are dirty, Father.'

The priest looked down, pretending to scratch his neck. He

did not look at Vitaly's pale eyes. *God's place is in the world, but the world is not God's place.* 'Bless you, my son.'

THE BISHOP: Dear Father Wajda,
They run through the streets of the ghetto here, killing, killing like you have never seen. It is terrible, some of it I cannot bear to describe. . .slicing up little children with their bayonets, butchering old women, and other horrors. I cannot help thinking that it is as a result of the Godless Communism that they have had inflicted on them, but it is still truly monstrous. However, they want to be pious, and I have been able to make some confess that killing in the ghetto is a sin of commission. These then only kill when the Germans tell them to. . .and as you know, the Germans do not suffer to have their orders disobeyed. Only last week I saw a Ukrainian refuse to shoot a Jewish child. He waved his arms and said the child could not be a Bolshevist. The German who gave the order to kill took out his Mauser and shot both the Ukrainian and the child. It was terrible. These Ukrainians want to be generous, and give large tithes to the Church. It is blood money, I know, but ownership of the thirty pieces of silver does not prevent us from using it to work for the Lord. . .You have one of those beastly German establishments in your district. The staff will be Ukrainian. Ask them to help with the orphanage. They will give generously of their ill-gotten wages. Yours in Christ Jesus. . .

'YOUR WORK will be rewarded in heaven.'
'Thank you, Father.'
'When you have made your gifts, you should come to the orphanage and see the fruits of your labour.'
'We will, Father.'
Magda encircled Vitaly's waist with one arm and kissed

his cheek. 'Ihor wants a hug from Daddy,' she said. 'And then he wants to go home.' Vitaly lifted his son to his face, fitting the baby's head gently into his large hand. Ihor responded by grabbing his father's nose and squawking. Father Wajda gazed intently at this scene of such domestic harmony for some moments before he realised that he was staring. He apologised, then hurried away to attend to other priestly duties.

'Dear Jesus,' he said later, on his knees, sweating before his Lord, 'I have tried to bring God and goodness to these people, tried to make them wash daily, send their children to school, love their neighbours. But they will not! They will not! Forgive me for using things from a German death camp to maintain our orphanage. . .Oh Lord, grant me absolution, without asking why!'

He bolted into the vestry, where the consecrated wine was kept. He withdrew a bottle, brushed away the layers of cobwebs and dust, then searched around in the gloom for a corkscrew. Sweaty beads of heat and terror popped out on his brow.

THE MAN and the woman took turns at pushing an English style pram. The man kept bending down to the child within. The woman did all the shopping when they were together. 'He's happy,' she said of her cooing husband, looking at the Warsaw salesgirl who happened to be serving her. 'It's a lovely child,' the girl said. 'Beautiful eyes. How old? Only six weeks.'

Was it not a beautiful portrait, the handsome man and the pretty woman and the child? Vitaly took his family to Warsaw to have its picture taken. The photographer remembered Vitaly. 'You've put on some weight. Voronikov has too? Good to see you. War not going as well as it could be. Hope those communists don't come to Poland. They'll ruin Poland. Your people are sorting out those ghetto Jews well enough. We stand on our roofs and watch. It's a good light show. Please sit there, madam. Look this way, sir. Head down a little, sir, or the flash will reflect off your glasses. Nice glasses, where did you get them?'

'At work. Only last week. I'm short-sighted. Always wanted gold frames.'

'Makes you look a scholar.'

'A scholar?'

'A university undergraduate, sir.'

'University? I never went to school. My brother did. My brother is at the front. Soon I will go to the front.'

'Shh, Vitaly, don't say that. I want Ihor to have a father!'

'Madam, please look this way. Yes. Good.'

VITALY walked down the path that led to the banks of the river Bug, his arms fanned out almost horizontally, his hands flicking the leaves and grasses on each side of the path. Magda followed a few paces behind, Ihor in her arms. The infant made appreciative gurgling noises as the soft sun fell in luminously golden dapples across his cheeks. Vitaly stopped and looked at the shining river. Magda draped his arm around her shoulders. He squeezed her and squinted. 'What a beautiful day,' he said. He noticed these things, she saw. The special powder-blue of the sky, the yellow and green grasses of spring. A row of pine trees lined the bank at regular intervals, and he sat beneath one, drawing his knees up to his chest.

He whipped out a cigarette in his neat way. He smoked Plaske brand, quite refined and expensive. He had smoked three on the short walk from the farm to the river. 'I hope the birds don't shit on me,' he said. The sun reflected off his glasses and turned them into two silver discs, making him eyeless for an instant. Magda seated herself comfortably on her long skirt and began breastfeeding Ihor. Vitaly leaned against the trunk of the tree and watched in silence, smoking another cigarette. She looked into the distance over Vitaly's shoulder and saw the head of a scoop-shovel dip and claw at the earth, then rise with its mouth full of something. Dirt, she supposed. An ugly plume of black smoke rose into the still air, refusing to dissipate. 'What are you *doing* in there? It stinks. Worse than ever before.'

Vitaly scratched at the banana-coloured earth beneath his feet with a twig. 'Burning stuff,' he mumbled. 'Burning Jews.'

'I thought so.'

'You don't mind?'

'As if I didn't know.'

'We only buried 'em, you see, and Himmler didn't like that.'

'It's a bad business. The Germans are shameful people.'

'It'll be finished soon.'

She looked at Ihor. 'Greedy boy! Finished already? You're just like your father.' She moved so that he could suckle from her other breast.

'The Germans might send me to the front.'

'Don't talk about it. If I'm going to lose you, I may as well enjoy you while I've got you. No point being gloomy.'

'Do you really love me, Magda Maria?' he asked, chuckling, and leaned over playfully, hands across his heart. She put her hands on her hips, her naked breasts swinging gently from side to side. Ihor gurgled.

'I live with you, don't I?' She wanted to be stern, but his giggling was infectious, and she joined in. He looked at her, blond hair falling over his eyes.

'I'm going for a swim. It's so hot. You know, sometimes the Germans let us come for a swim.'

'Don't even mention the Germans to me.'

He had stripped off his calico shirt, and was in the process of removing his socks when she said 'Take everything off. I want to see you in broad daylight.'

'There's a word for people like you,' he said, obliging her. He dived into the silver river, his long sleek body disturbing the pine tree reflections. He stayed under for what seemed an eternity, then burst through the surface, blowing and sputtering.

'You silly sausage,' she yelled. 'You've left your specs on.' He grinned, then swam over to the bank and passed them into her outstretched hand. 'You come in for a bit. I'll mind Ihor.' He clambered up the steep bank and sat on his shirt. She shed her long skirt and full blouse, and stepped in gingerly. 'Coward!' he called after her. 'It's better when you dive in.'

'Oh, shush.' She ducked her head briefly, then paddled over to a smooth, round rock in the middle of the stream. She dragged herself onto it, then raised her arms above her head. 'I'm a damsel in distress,' she yelled.

Vitaly stretched out close beside his sated son, covering him with a sleeve of his shirt and giving him a finger to play with. He wrinkled his nose. 'And I'm a father in distress, because a certain little boy has just shit himself.'

'Bring him in. We can wash him, and the water will do him good.'

THE MAN and the woman naked in the water, with a five months old baby between them. The sky arching above, fringed by pines and shrubs. The man will go to the front, the woman will stay. The baby will grow up in the new Poland, the man will go to the new country, the woman will finally accept her lot, but that is many years away. The woman's hair fans out in the water. The baby grabs it. The father swims around them. He says, 'The hair on your legs is the same colour as the hair on your head.' The sun shines from a kindly sky. They do not hear the sound of the scoop-shovel over the water splashes, and they choose to ignore the plume of black smoke.

MAGDA: 'I suppose it had to come, but I hated it, and not just me, the whole town, but for different reasons. The Germans shut Treblinka. There was a revolt in the concentration camp—oh, it was terrible. Half the prisoners escaped, and there were big shoot-outs. I heard that some of the Ukrainians gave the Jews guns, because they were fed up with the Germans. They have a devil inside them, the Germans, because they are clever with it. The Germans started to lose the war, but they wouldn't admit it. Some of the Ukrainians said it was wrong to kill Jews from Poland, because they were not Bolshevists. Berik would have helped the Jews in the revolt, but he was afraid for his woman. The Germans were not above killing a man's wife if he disobeyed. I know that Franz shot one of the Ukrainians, Pavel Stashytsyn, because Pavel said that Treblinka was a giant sin that the Germans would have to pay for in Hell. Pavel Stashytsyn stood right up in the main street, yelling at Kurt Franz, 'You are going to Hell, I am going to Hell, the Reich is going to Hell. You've made your own Hell. HELL!' I had a sudden vision of Kurt Franz with a trident in his hand, and I saw two bumps on his bumpy forehead grow into curved horns. But his trident was really his rifle and he used it to shoot Pavel Stashytsyn straight through the heart.

I know Vitaly was getting afraid of the Germans as well. He told me some of the things that happened there. The camp was a shameful place. But it did bring prosperity to our village, and you shouldn't complain about prosperity, or you get the opposite, you know—the Evil Eye. Bad times.

I think the revolt happened when a whole lot of Ukrainians and a couple of the Germans went for a swim in the river, and there weren't enough guards in the camp. Summer was so hot, that year. One Jew came to our house, the doctor with the big nose. Vitaly was supposed to be searching in Małkinia, people were running everywhere, it was crazy. I was at home with Ihor and the little kids. The doctor didn't look evil, he was just scared. At the time I didn't know what was good or right, although now people say I was very brave and right. I told him how to get away. I told him he could fight with the *Armia Krajowa*, the Polish partisans, who sometimes hid in the far woods, but he said he did not want to fight for anything, he just wanted to be a doctor. I don't think the doctor killed anyone. He was nice. He said I was a 'virtuous gentile', whatever that means. But I'm pleased Papa wasn't there. He would have given him to the Germans.

Soon after the Jew doctor had run away, Vitaly came to the house all red in the face and sweating and panting. He took off his cap and threw it on the floor and swore at the Germans, terrible swear words. He held up his index finger and yelled, 'I am a man, a man, not a monster' as much at himself as anyone. He stomped around the house, yelling all the time. Then he started to cry and slid down our bedroom wall. Next thing, his eyes rolled up in his head, and he stared white and blind at me. I asked him. 'What do you want?' and he answered me, 'I don't know.' He sucked his thumb like a little child, sobbing 'bastards bastards bastards.' I had never seen a man act like that before. I think at that moment he realised that it wasn't just the Germans and the communists, it was him too.

Quite a few of the Ukrainians were killed; I remember Voronikov was killed, the top of his head was shot off. One of the yellow men, Tsieh Shura, he was killed too. I found out that the Germans killed him, though, not the Jews. He gave one of the Jews some ammunition, like Berik, only he got caught doing it. Ivan M. the footballer ran all through our town with Ivan the Terrible looking for people, but my little doctor had long gone. Vitaly was asleep on our bed. I could believe that Ivan the Terrible was mad after that; one Jew that he caught, he twisted his head clean off his shoulders and left it in the street. It sat there for three hours, grinning at us, until the Germans came and cleaned the street. Berik Houmenko was killed also, and Nikolai was shot in the arm, and his wife was crying and upset. Poor Berik. He hated Treblinka and the Germans but he did what he was told and got killed. It was a shame. So the Germans shut the camp, and sent the Ukrainians to the front, or to Italy. Oh, all we women were crying and wailing. One of the Germans came down in his black car. He said to stop all this Slavic carry-on, he said we breed like rabbits anyway. Only Nikolai was allowed to take his wife and family with him to Italy, but she looked scared. I don't know why. He seemed a good husband. Then the Germans levelled the site and planted baby pine trees all over it. Vitaly called such business 'German happy horseshit'. I'm ashamed to say that many of our villagers went and dug up the baby pine trees, searching for gold and valuables, plucking the ground to pieces, so the Germans had to come back and replant them all and put guards there. I pleaded with the Germans to let Vitaly stay, or to allow us to stay together, but that bastard Franz, the one who shot Pavel, he threatened to shoot anyone who complained. The Germans said that the Askaris would come back from the front, but they never did. The Germans couldn't hold out even for that long. I've since heard that Vitaly went to Australia. I wish I went to Australia, Ihor did a project on it at school. It seems a nice place, lots of sunshine. Vitaly would like it there.'

THE GERMANS let the Ukrainians say farewell to their Polish womenfolk for a week: they found it amusing. The Poles and Ukrainians were infected with what Stangl and most of the Germans considered a peculiarly Slavic despondency, which they stoked with vodka. Ukrainians wove irregularly through the town, smashing things and fighting each other. Magda saw one of them kneeling in a field of rye, his hands raised above his head, shaking from alcoholic torpor. The sky stretching away indefinitely hard and steely, the field yellow and green. His rifle was in front of him. Two little children watched him wail; they stood hand in hand on the other side of the grey strip of road. They watched his arms rise and flap helplessly, like the wings of some monstrous bird, eternally frustrated by its failure to fly.

She said to Vitaly, 'You will never come back.'

He said, 'No. Never.'

'Kiss your son. Remember me.'

He swore that he would devote what remained of his life to the memory of Magda and Ihor. For a very long time he kept his word.

Did he cry? Could such a man be deemed capable of crying? Of course he did. The Germans loaded the Ukrainians onto lorries near the concentration camp site, and cordoned off the villagers. They shot two of them, and Vitaly heard one of the Germans say, 'They're only Poles. Two less won't do any harm.' Vitaly saw women holding up small children and crying hysterically. He cried too; so did Ivan the Terrible and Mohammed Yerlan Tian. But their tears were from a cauterised place, not like the women's tears. Stangl stared at the wailing women and their offspring and shook his head. 'Look,' he murmured. 'They have peopled the whole island with Calibans.' Nikolai nursed his sore arm. Vitaly concentrated on Magda's white face, but saw instead a pile of bodies the communists left in the middle of the collective at one stage during the famine, gathered behind the iron gate. The gate loomed up in front of his nose, and he focused on the blond boy standing in front of the bodies. The boy was naked, his hands forming a pathetic figleaf in front of his penis. Blood ran from the boy's back, moistening the earth. He tried shutting his eyes, and Magda screamed. The lorries rumbled away.

FOUR

KATERYNA: I have only to taste the sweetness of condensed milk, and I remember the prisoner of war camp at Riccione. It was less of a home for prisoners than a place for the British to keep all the people who had no country any more. In Italy the summers are hot, and I remember how the storm-driven rain and wind would beat down on stuffy Nissen huts and on our battered wooden church. Families huddled in the huts, prayed in the church. *Please don't send us back to Russia. Stalin will kill us all.* The British let us Ukrainian women join our husbands and brothers, or, failing that, let us join our own people again; just listening to the chatter of familiar syllables repeated over and over was comforting. The British did not know what to do with us; we were displaced, disempowered folk.

In 1945 an entire division of Waffen SS surrendered to the British at Klagenfurt in Austria. This was the 14th Waffen SS Galizien Division, an entirely Ukrainian division, in which my brother Evheny served. The British did not know what nationality they were, or considered them Polish, so they sent them to Italy, to Riccione, south of Rimini, on the Adriatic coast. Ukrainians scattered all over Europe joined them, and it was here that I found my brother, whom I had not seen since 1941.

At first the British sent all the Ukrainians and Cossacks

they captured back to the Soviet Union, under the terms of the treaty of Yalta. They sent them back in trains and on ships. The NKVD would be waiting with their machine-guns, and they would be shot en masse at the border. Forty thousand Cossacks were killed in this way, and many other people. Kalmyks and Kazakhs. The British did not want them, because they looked strange, and would not be good British subjects. Perhaps because the British discovered that Stalin shot all the people repatriated to the Soviet Union, perhaps because they felt sorry for us, the Ukrainians in Italy were spared repatriation. Others were less fortunate. In one camp in Belgium, five hundred Ukrainians committed collective suicide when they heard that they were to be returned to Stalin. I also remember Russians and others who had spent the war labouring without wages in German factories, or in prisoner of war camps, being dragged away by British soldiers to transports that would take them back to Russia. Sometimes the ordinary British soldiers would object, and would cry and argue with their officers, but they had to do as they were told. I remember one Kazakh who cut his wrists in protest, and wrapped himself up in the British flag. The British commander stepped over the body when he came out to eat breakfast the next morning. He seemed unworried. He had been in the Imperial Service in Burma.

Evheny was wounded: a Russian bullet had shattered his shin. Vitaly was gone, apparently forever. The British needed labourers for their factories and their farms, domestics for their hospitals and homes, so they planned to take us to Britain. They told us if we were 'well behaved', they would let us become British subjects. This meant something. It was valuable. When Soviet missions came to Riccione, trying to retrieve former Soviet citizens as fodder for Stalinist public executions, the British told us how to evade their questions. They did not want any more suicides, or a repeat of the situation with the Cossacks. They said, 'You tell them you all come from Polish West Ukraine, not Soviet Ukraine. Then they can't have you. You were coerced into the German ranks. You want to emigrate. Anything'. It was partly true. Many Ukrainians came from Poland. Many Ukrainians were coerced into the Waffen SS. One man I met was beaten by the Germans with a sword because he refused to shoot some runaway Jews. 'Like the Germans?' He yelled. 'I'd like to kick their arses!' He shot the required number of Jews when the Germans threatened his wife. I asked, 'How many?' He said, 'Seven hundred and fifty. I see things, but I can't feel anything now. Not good or bad.' He smiled grimly.

Evheny sometimes spoke about the past:

'When I was ten, the commies caught me stealing food from their stores. I was going to be publicly flogged. My brother Vitaly came forward and took my punishment, you know. He couldn't walk for two weeks. He just took it. They cut him to pieces. Then when I was in the SS we got attacked by NKVD and I was lying down and all these dead bodies were on top of me. I could smell blood and plums, part of it was in a plum orchard, and all these NKVD were up there prodding around with their bayonets to see if anyone was alive and I just couldn't move. I was there for nine fucking hours until the SS retook the position and I was nearly off my head when they got me out of there.'

They only talked like this when they were drunk. Mostly they were silent. I noticed that my brother muttered in his sleep, but he would not answer any questions about the war, no matter how gently I asked.

At last the British saved our lives, and we were grateful. We were to be taken to Britain. We did not know why they had changed their minds, and were too frightened to ask. Kind Britons came to the camp and told us about cricket and democracy; this was called 'The British Government and Way of Life.' They explained that we could leave for the colonies if we did not like Britain; Canada and Australia needed settlers. Evheny was baffled when one of the British people showed him a globe of the world. Britain fitted into Canada and Australia many times over, yet it owned these vast places.

The British fixed Evheny's leg, gave my children inoculations. I began to love the British. But what of my other love, Captain Wilhelm Hasse? I married him. He took me most places with him, even to Treblinka, where Vitaly served. I didn't see Vitaly. Willie said it probably would not have been possible. I met his stiff and religious family, and accepted Willie's explanation for their behaviour: 'They are like many Germans, they have ice, not blood, flowing in their veins.' He gave me two beautiful children, and was killed in the battle for Stalingrad. The Germans sent me his medals in a little velvet box, and I received a consoling telegram from Hitler. 'Your husband was outstanding in his bravery for the Reich.' When he was gone, I asked myself what I saw in him. The telegram said he was killed trying to lead a group of soldiers through the Russian encirclement. So perhaps he was brave, whatever that means. My daughter from my second marriage, Siobhan, says it is all right now for a woman to admit that she married a man simply because she was attracted to him. Sexually. And that was why I married Willie. When I stepped out of the shower that first time in Kiev, admiring the lovely dress he had given me, he was sitting naked on the edge of the bed with his cock sticking right up. He said, 'Before you wear that, I want to fuck you.' At first I was repelled, but when he touched me—with his hand, I think it was—I wanted to sleep with him so badly I couldn't control myself. I suppose he truly was a wicked bastard. He was cruel and clever at the same time. But when he kissed me, I couldn't think about what he was or what he did. And when he was killed, I woke up in a different world. I worried about the family I had forgotten for three years.

In time, I discovered that my mother had been deported to Germany in June 1943 as part of a forced labour contingent.

The Germans sometimes uprooted whole Ukrainian villages and used the people as labourers in their munitions plants. They always promised to return the people to their homes, but they never did. As an unpaid *Ostarbeiter*, my mother's work conditions would not have been good. I learned that she died in an industrial accident. She was electrocuted. I could discover no more. I remember hating the Germans. While her two sons were helping the Germans, and her daughter was married to one, she was dying from shock in a Siemens factory. Shortly after I learnt this, the Vatican sent Archbishop Buchko to Riccione to minister to the Ukrainian flock. I confessed my hate to him. He shook his head, sighing. 'We will never heal the past. Never. It is too late.'

About Vitaly I could learn nothing. Evheny and I assumed he was dead. It was only in 1949, when I was working as a European Voluntary Worker at a nursery in Surrey, and Evheny and his British fiancée, Margaret Collins, were planning to emigrate to Canada, that we learned where he was.

He sent a letter addressed to me. It came from Bonegilla, Victoria, Australia. The stamp bore a comforting portrait of the gentle English king. At first, I was afraid to open the envelope. I turned it over and over in my hands. Finally, I rode at a furious pace down to Margaret's to share my missive with Evheny, rattling and bumping over the cobblestones, my teeth shaking in my head. I rode past the common with the English children playing cricket and slipping through the air on swings. Past the green verge that led into the Farmer's Arms. Past the row of poplars with their golden leaves. 'My brother! My brother is alive!' Evheny and I had been in England three years now. Vitaly, we learned, had been in Australia only six months. The letter was typewritten, obviously the product of several hours' labour. But he had written it. Later, I understood that this was all that mattered.

Dere Katya,
I know that you dont know where I are, but I are in Australia,

and I am being learned english here at Bonegilla. I will have a job soon building a power station. I come to Australia from Stuttgart at Xmas. It is hot here in Summer, and it is dusty. Here I am called Vic because they cant say Vitaly. The man here says you are in England Where is Evheny the man don;t know where he are. Please rite back to me I have put in some forms for you to come to Australia.

Very Truly Yours,
Vic Kovalenko.

I remember dropping the letter. Henry, Margaret's father, said I fainted away for *three whole hours*. I woke up in Margaret's bed, a doctor leaning over me, a thermometer under my tongue, sheets bunched around my neck. I listened to Margaret and Evheny's conversation echoing up the stairs. There was a change of plan. They were going to Australia. They won't have to give me English lessons, Evheny was saying. I'm a British Subject! Later, Henry brought Bernard and Anton from the nursery. Anton, my oldest, sat at the foot of my bed, legs folded. 'Can we go to Australia?' he asked. The image of his father. I saw it then, and cried. My first tears for twelve years. Since that communist beating, centuries ago. The tears flooded down my face and seemed to wash away the hate I had stored up inside myself. Henry, Evheny and Margaret took turns—like shifts—to sit by the bed as I cried. Eventually I ran out of tears, and went to sit in the copper bath. The bedsheets were soaked. Henry said, 'She dammed up her Ukrainian blood with a hate as daily as the papers.' I held my boys in my arms. Henry and ginger-haired Margaret stood over me. Evheny said, 'We will go.' I said, 'We will go.'

About an hour later, I went outside and burnt the Hitler telegram and buried the medals. The telegram made little carbonised flakes on the red gladioli, before landing on the soil, softly. I patted the earth down, and sat in the sun for a moment, beside Henry's roses. The light was soft, the garden smelled sweet and freshly mowed; the sounds of a Bach

concerto, picked out inexpertly on piano keys floated upwards
and outwards.

'DOES IT hurt, to remember?'

'Yes, because I thought I could stop thinking but I can't.
You keep thinking. It either goes out or stays in.'

'With Bret it came out.'

'Yes. It came out, and made him sick. With me it stayed in,
and made me sick. But then, it was a very sick thing to do.'

'You think that?'

'Yes. Even then, it was sick. It was doing the same thing
back at them. You know.'

'Back and forth, like a pendulum.'

'Like that, only a clock winds down. People don't wind
down. They just go on.'

'I learnt that at school. The only thing you learn is that you
never learn.'

'Like that. But I can read now. I can see. When you can't
read, you're blind. Not even a dog to guide you.'

'I can't imagine that. No writing. No speech. Like having
your tongue cut out.'

'The flow passes out between your lips but other people
can't hear it. Only you can hear it. It buzzes in your ears and
won't let you rest but no one else can hear it. Or you. It hurts.
Can you see my letter?'

'What letter?'

'The letter I was writing to you. Is it there. . .under the
inkwell?'

'Yes. It's here. I've got it safe under the inkwell. It's all
together. Everything remembered.'

'Good. It's important. You mustn't misplace it.'

'Did you want anything. . .in the beginning, even? More
than the letter. . .more than you want anything now?'

'Yes, you know, you always want things. People want

things. I wasn't greedy, though. I only wanted to be left alone. To lie still. On my farm, where I would grow the finest wheat and bake the best bread and my wife would make the best *cutleti* and *piroshki* in all Ukraine.'

'Your wife?'

'My wife Ulrike. She would have been a good wife, on a proper farm, in a real village. Not the collective. On my farm. That's what I wanted, if you want to know.'

'Didn't you want to be free?'

'No, not really. That is something that *you* want. I wanted calm and stillness, on my farm, in my place. This is your place; you have freedom here. In my place I wanted peace. Just peace, just to be left alone. If you leave people alone they don't do bad things.'

'But then you would never have come here. We wouldn't be here.'

'That's all right. You would want what others want. In a proper village, everyone wants things for everybody, not just for themselves. Here you have to want things for yourself. But that is all right too.'

'It depends on where you are.'

'Where your place is.'

'Are you worried about the trial?'

'Yes and no; yes because they will make me remember, try to make me explain why, or what I wanted. Why the hate. Why this, why that. I don't think I can explain. And also because they will not understand. And no because I like the lawyer. He is good-hearted. He tries to understand.'

'I still don't think we will learn anything.'

'Yes, yes, you are right. But they try. They are trying.'

'Are you trying? Trying. . .to be sorry? Are you sorry?'

'I am trying. It takes time, but I am trying. To be sorry.'

A HOSPITAL. They have painted the walls with bright murals, and the nurses smile now, but my feet still echo reluctantly along pale pastel corridors. The intensive care unit has high windows, daytime windows that would refract bright light prismatically into a hundred dark corners, but it is night and the light is sick and yellow. My family is gathered around the shrunken figure of Vitaly caged behind a latticework of plastic tubing. He is asleep. My father says, 'He told us not to blame you. You need to know.'

Staciya says, 'I only wish that I could die first.'

'He's not going to die! Don't be such. . .such fatalists!'

The room seems to disengage from my senses. I think of dreams. Maybe I am tired. 'He seems to want to die. He's had a hard life.' Mum is putting her arm around me. 'The doctor says he won't regain consciousness.'

'But you said——.'

'That was an hour and a half ago. He's willing himself off.'

'What did he say before he slept? Apart from not blaming me—anything?' She guides me out of the IC unit. We sit on vinyl chairs the colour of clay.

'Staciya must not hear. Not yet. She wasn't here. He shouted out a woman's name, over and over, and something in Polish. Evheny wouldn't tell me what it meant. "Magda! Magda! Ja umrze!" Something like that.'

' "Magda, I'm dying." That's what it means. Roughly. Magda was the woman he married in Poland. In the war.' I am crying. I say, 'It will be a relief to get his body in the ground. He wrote to Magda. I can tell her that he's going. Gone.'

My father pokes his head around the door. 'He's woken up. He wants a priest. The doctors are getting a priest.'

I feel sorry for Father O'Connor, when he comes. Vitaly loses his English, chattering in Ukrainian as the priest holds the crucifix forward for him to kiss. The priest prays softly, and Vitaly stops speaking, but his hands wander aimlessly over the sheet. The priest dips his thumb in the oil and begins to administer extreme unction: the scent of sanctified oil fills the room. The priest sits by the narrow bed, gently pushes the frame supporting the drip to one side. He tells Vitaly how he must abandon himself to divine mercy. The doctor, a young man, unused to religious ritual, shifts his weight uneasily on the balls of his feet. Vitaly closes his eyes. His face is gentle. The doctor moves closer, bending over, looking at the silent instruments beside Vitaly's head. The priest is on his knees now, praying. His purple stole is draped across the still figure.

I recalled that peaceful death mask numerous times in the summer that followed. I graduated with it. I went overseas, searched out its origins. The extended family members talked, each to the other.

'Took the Church on his deathbed?'

'So Staciya says.'

'He'll have business to attend to in purgatory before he sees the Lord.'

'I'll say.'

'Staciya all right?'

'Seems so. She's living with his brother.'

I heard only some of the gossip as I completed my own tasks: writing to Magda on the family's behalf, finishing my studies. The talk and the travel and the mask made up the pieces of my quiet life. The war crimes trials came and went, came and went. I wrote letters to various Australian newspapers and magazines, protesting against the trials. But my father was never charged, and I concentrated on other things. I took a Russian subject in second semester. It seemed sensible.

AT TREBLINKA itself, as Vitaly told me, nothing remains. Even the memorial is poorly kept, now no communist regime needs it for moral capital. Long grass sprouts between the paving stones. Broken clumps of rock recall the various Jewish communities exterminated there. Carved into the largest piece of rock are the words 'Never Again' in Polish, Russian and

English. The smaller slabs of rock have been deliberately cut into irregular shapes. A neat obelisk would not do here. Each shape bears the name of a town. The pines are still there, those as yet uncleared, at least. While I am walking towards the memorial, a Trabant with unified Germany numberplates clatters past. It sports a new bumper sticker—*My other car is also a piece of shit*. The car shudders to a stop. The driver, a young man with black curly hair, leans across and opens the door. We drive to the site, to the pines and broken rocks. He says, 'My aunt died here.' I say, 'My uncle was a guard here.'

I ask, 'Why?'

He says, 'She was a Quaker. A pacifist. She couldn't fight so she hid Jews from the authorities. Eventually they caught her. They said if you want to be friendly with Jews, we'll make you into a Jew. And?'

'My uncle? He volunteered. He was a poor peasant.'

He looks at me, sharply, but not angrily. 'Are you sorry?'

'Yes,' I said. 'I am.'

'Is he?'

'He's dead.'

'Too late to ask him now.'